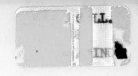

D1154237

A Garland Series

Classics of Children's Literature 1621-1932

A collection of 117 titles
reprinted in photo-facsimile
in 73 volumes

Selected and arranged by
Alison Lurie
and
Justin G. Schiller

Two Little Confederates

Thomas Nelson Page

and

The Little Colonel

Annie Fellows Johnston

with a preface
for the Garland edition by

Sarah Elbert

Garland Publishing, Inc., New York & London

1976

Bibliographical note:

The facsimile of
Two Little Confederates
has been made from a copy
in the possession of the Publishers.

The facsimile of
The Little Colonel
has been made from a copy
in the possession
of Justin G. Schiller, Ltd.

Library of Congress Cataloging in Publication Data

Page, Thomas Nelson, 1853-1922.
Two little Confederates.

(Classics of children's literature, 1621-1932)
Reprint of the 1888 ed. of Two little Confederates published by Scribner, New York, and of the 1896 ed. of The Little Colonel published by J. Knight, Boston, issued in series: Cozy corner series.
Includes bibliographies.
SUMMARY: The first of these two novels presents a boy's-eye view of the Civil War from the southern side. In the second a spunky little girl reunites a fragmented family after the Civil War.
1. United States--History--Civil War, 1861-1865--Juvenile fiction. [1. United States--History--Civil War, 1861-1865--Fiction]
I. Johnston, Annie Fellows, 1863-1931. The Little Colonel. 1976. II. Title. III. Series.
PZ7.P145Tw26 [Fic] 76-29926
ISBN 0-8240-2305-6

Printed in the United States of America

Preface

Edmund Wilson once said that "it was hard to make the Civil War seem cosy, but Thomas Nelson Page did his best."[1] Born on a small plantation in Oakland, Virginia, in 1853, Page's boyhood closely paralleled the romantic world of *The Two Little Confederates.* As the impoverished descendant of a Page he recalled as "the wealthiest gentleman in Virginia," a confidante of Jefferson, T.N. Page turned to writing as a means of defending his heritage and escaping the confines of a small-town law practice. He dedicated the greater part of his life and literary career to defending the Old South and its culture against the dominant industrial North.

In *The Two Little Confederates,* which appeared in 1888 in the *St. Nicholas Magazine,* Page himself undertook the charge he had placed upon "the future historian of the Old South." Childhood and adolescence had gained enormous importance in the antebellum years as rapid changes dislocated traditional institutions of stability and socialization. The family alone seemed to retain integrity, indeed seemed even to gain in prestige and power and hold the salvation of the Republic. For Page and other defenders of the old order the threat of change brought a renewed effort to recreate, in fiction, the secure world they had once known. That world, Page argued, "preserved the spirit of civil and religious liberty pure and undefiled, and established it as the guiding star of the American people forever." He reminded an audience at the University of Virginia that "Both Grant and Lincoln—the great general and the still greater President—sprang from Southern loins." The Civil War was to him not only as senseless and inhuman but also as glorious as it appeared to the two little confederates, Frank and Willy.

He saw Northern abolitionism as a seditious plot to incite slave insurrections and put a bloody halt to the gradual and peaceful emancipation initiated by the slaveholders. Slavery itself was not the hideous misery depicted in Northern novels, but rather the rational paternalism of Oakland. Southerners had reluctantly accepted the white man's burden and brought Christianity and civilization to the savage Africans, whose brutal middle passage had largely profited pious

Northern capitalists. Indeed, as Page described it slavery was "the automatic balance wheel between labor and capital which prevented, on the one hand, the excessive accumulation of wealth, with its attendant perils, and on the other hand prevented" the growth of "the immense pauper class which work[s] for less than the wage of the slave without any of his incidental compensations."[2]

Frank and Willy learn the unquestioned and "natural" hierarchy of the world in miniature at Oakland. It is a chivalric pageant dominated by the shaping of Southern white manhood; the boys' father, a warrior knight, has a faithful body slave who follows him in the service of the doomed but noble Cause. Hugh, page and then squire to Colonel Marshall, is eventually knighted himself on the field of valor. The knights' ladies are reminiscent of the heroines of *Ivanhoe*, a favorite novel of antebellum Southern cavaliers. Belle is a fashionable flirt, but marriage will transform her into the mistress of a plantation and like Frank and Willy's mother she will be a maternal angel to all the creatures in her care.

The boys' path to manhood is essentially one of individual and brotherly adherence to a stern code of duty, honor, valor, and courtesy. Their models are white male relatives and the mythic heroes who represent their culture's ideal types. The little Negro boys are permanent squires, perhaps the future body servants of the young knights-to-be. Uncle Balla is their companion, honored by their mother above other servants as the real-life Uncle Balla was honored by Page in essays, lectures, and novels. But when Uncle Balla attempts to show the boys how a "man" does a job, he degenerates into a comic Sambo figure who has experience in commanding horses but not men. He is perpetually astounded at the daring and intelligence of the boys; they will grow to manhood while Uncle Balla for all his faithful service must remain a childlike dependent.

In a stunning rejoinder to Northern abolitionism Page has Lucy, the black nursemaid, outwit Union soldiers searching for Hugh and Colonel Marshall by pretending to covet her freedom. When she snuffs out her candle, only she and the rebel fugitives know what is really happening. Lucy's ruse enables the Rebels to escape, but it is Frank and Willy's fulfillment of the Code which ensures their safety. Their bravery so impresses the Northern soldiers that one gentle Yankee is led to treat Frank as his own son. The gentle trooper is killed, and it is the shared mothers' grief that makes reunification possible. The boys have fulfilled the ultimate obligation of the Code. Their reward will be the gift of those sidearms laid down at Appomatox and generously returned by Grant to the Confederate officers. Even more telling is the way the boys receive the finest weapons the Northern gunsmiths can produce from the hands of a Northern widow and orphan eager to believe in the nobility of the Old South. With her arms and honor restored both the War and Reconstruction are over and the period Southern writers termed "Redemption" is at hand.

Thomas Nelson Page had an enormously successful career, not only because he was steeped in the chivalry so dear to Southern literary tradition but also because he thoroughly understood and shared "the mind of the South." His first wife, Anne Selden Bruce, who died a few years after their marriage, was the model for Southern womanhood in his novels, and the slaves of his family and friends were carefully transferred to fiction as their masters saw them. In 1893 Page married Mrs. Florence S. Field, the rich, widowed sister-in-law of Marshall Field, and left Virginia for Washington. He regarded public office, like the military, as the service a Southern gentleman owed his country; and Woodrow Wilson, receptive to his nomination by Virginia senators, appointed Page ambassador to Italy in 1913. He held the post for six years and was a great success, aiding Italian war-relief efforts and finally writing a social history, *Italy and the World War,* in 1920. Italy was, for him, a defeated nation reminiscent of his Old South.

To the end Page remained the champion of what he thought were the highest and noblest ideals of Anglo-Saxon manhood and womanhood, and he defended them in many novels and essays against the crass commercial spirit he saw pervading America. If Page's view of American society and particularly of the "Negro question" was a controversial one in his youth, it had become widely shared by the time of his death in 1922 at Oakland. A romantic nostalgia for the Old South and particularly for the imaginary lost childhood of an entire nation brought tears to the eyes of a generation who may not have read *Two Little Confederates* but who received its message in later films and novels—particularly in the children's story which became a hit film starring Shirley Temple and Bojangles Robinson, *The Little Colonel.*

In Annie Fellows Johnston's novel *The Little Colonel,* the flowering of young manhood gives way to a Redemption of quite a new sort. Mrs.

Johnston also believed in the Biblical prophecy "a little child shall lead them," but her girl-child was a purely postbellum phenomenon, unlike any known to the world of *The Two Little Confederates.*

Annie Fellows was born in 1863 in Evansville, Indiana, the descendant of Massachusetts Methodists who had emigrated to the Midwest two generations earlier. Her childhood was as pastoral and family centered as any in the early nineteenth century, but there was a difference. Education had opened up for many young women in the postwar period and school teaching and office work were becoming increasingly respectable for unmarried middle-class girls. Moreover, Annie Fellows's maternal grandfather, though a slaveowner, had emancipated his slaves in Maryland and moved first to Kentucky and then to Indiana. A sturdy faith in democracy, education, and reform marked the entire family. When their father died the mother built a house on the family farm and reared her three daughters in a vigorous religious and intellectual environment. Annie Fellows published her first poem when she was sixteen, was teaching district school by seventeen, and had a year at the University of Iowa before she went to work as a private secretary for three years.

When she finally married a widowed cousin, William Johnston, she found a ready audience for her children's stories in her three stepchildren. She sent the stories off to the *Youth's Companion* and saw them printed. But as chance would have it her avocation became a serious career when her husband died just three years after their marriage. By 1894 his wife had published her first book, *Big Brother.* Then, competing for a religious organization's prize, she wrote *Joel: A Boy of Galilee.* A visit to the Pewee Valley of Kentucky inspired *The Little Colonel,* and its success inspired twelve more novels about its heroine, Lloyd Sherman. Lloyd's fictional friend, Mary Ware, even acquired a literary life of her own in *Mary Ware, The Little Colonel's Chum* (1908).

Lloyd Sherman introduced not only Page's Old Colonel but an enthusiastic young audience to the New South. If Thomas Nelson Page had held himself aloof from the regional champions of this new social phenomenon, Northern and Southern moderates were well represented by Annie Fellows Johnston. She too applauded public education as the solution to the "Negro Problem" and expanding business developments in the West as the solution to the myth of the lazy South. In her most famous book she joined the Old South and the North in the marriage of Elizabeth Lloyd, daughter of the Old Colonel, and Jack Sherman. Their child, Lloyd Sherman, is remarkable not only for her successful efforts to reunite a fragmented family, emblematic of the war-torn nation, but also for her own character and new gender role. If her mother has never been known to step outside her own bedroom unshod, little Lloyd joyously wiggles her toes in the dust, "just like a little nigger." And her espousal of that race does not end with bare feet.

She finds Black playmates and proceeds to teach them the art of mudpies and the morals of Billy Goat Gruff. Black and white children had certainly played together in the Old South and Lloyd Sherman as clearly continued to dominate May Lilly, but there are equally clear indications that the cook's child is bright and may not long remain ignorant. Faithful Mom Beck is superstitious like Uncle Balla, but she is a larger person, clearly adult. It is in fact her white mistress, Elizabeth Lloyd Sherman, who appears childlike and dependent upon Mom Beck. Southern white womanhood had not the same mystique for a Midwestern working widow as it had for a gentleman of the Old South; Thomas Nelson Page and Colonel Lloyd shared the same world view.

Lloyd Sherman has inherited her mother's hazel eyes but also her grandfather's ferocious temper, and adults seem alternately amused and cowed by her bids for power over her own life. In some sense it is the New Woman who conquers the Old South in *The Little Colonel.* Lloyd loves flowers and pink and blue stories, but she also hates being a little lady and quite manfully decides to accept punishment rather than limit her freedom to roam the neighborhood, barefoot. If Lloyd's Mama is helpless and exhausted from the first real work of her life, her daughter shows signs of inexhaustible energy and self will. Despite her youth and gender, Lloyd's view of the world is far more sophisticated than that of Frank and Willy. In a certain sense she must create her own code, not only because she seeks to unite two different cultures but because she also seeks to transcend the limitations of her femininity.

The solution to the imagined (and partially real) financial woes that impinge on a child's happiness lies in the West. It is Westward expansion that Johnston credits for the recoupment of fortunes lost in the recurrent failures of the speculative and often disastrous business cycles of the postwar period. Shrewdly she notes that it is not just hard work but luck and the right family connections that help put Jack

Sherman back on his feet financially and physically. If the larger world is precarious, there is still the reassurance of "Locust." The plantation survives magically, its gilded harp untarnished and its candles lit once more to welcome the reunited family. If love of the little Colonel, the innocent child who must not suffer for the sins of her parents or grandparents, reunites North and South, it seems somehow a fragile, even sorrowful, reunion. The Colonel struggles, we are told, between love and pride, and only his loss of both wife and son lead him to humble himself to recover "his own."

Annie Fellows Johnston knew the limits of her heroines' lives and the limits of her female readers' lives as well. In some fifty books her heroines always ended their lives with marriage. As moral guides to growing up in America her works could not, even by her death in 1931, recommend a path for the "New Woman" beyond that great event in her life.

Sarah Elbert

SARAH ELBERT is an Assistant Professor of History and Director of Special Programs at the State University of New York at Binghamton. She has written and lectured widely on the history of education and is the author of the forthcoming The Sad Sisterhood: Louisa May Alcott and the Woman Problem.

Notes

1. Edmund Wilson, *Patriotic Gore* (New York 1962), pp. 613-614.
2. Thomas Nelson Page, *The Old South: Essays Social and Political* (Volume 7 of *Works*) (New York 1906), p. 52.

THOMAS NELSON PAGE (1853-1922)

Bibliography of His Books for Children:

Two Little Confederates. New York 1888.

Among the Camps. New York 1891.

Pastime Stories. New York 1894.

Selected References:

Page, Rosewell. *Thomas Nelson Page: A Memoir of a Virginia Gentleman.* New York 1923.

Gross, Theodore L. *Thomas Nelson Page.* New York 1967.

ANNIE FELLOWS JOHNSTON (1863-1931)

Bibliography of Her Books for Children:

Big Brother. Boston 1893.

Joel—A Boy of Galilee. Boston 1895.

The Little Colonel. Boston 1895.

Old Mammy's Torment. Boston 1897.

Songs Ysame. (Poems written with her sister, Mrs. Albion Fellows Bacon.) Boston 1897.

The Giant Scissors. Boston [c. 1898].

The Little Colonel Stories. Boston [c. 1899].

Two Little Knights of Kentucky. Boston 1899.

The Little Colonel's House Party. Boston 1900.

The Story of Dago. Boston 1900.

The Little Colonel's Holidays. Boston 1901.

Asa Holmes; or, At the Cross-roads. Boston 1902.

The Little Colonel's Hero. Boston 1902.

Cicely, and Other Stories. Boston 1903.

The Little Colonel at Boarding School. Boston 1903.

Aunt Liza's Hero, and Other Stories. Boston 1904.

Flip's "Islands of Providence." Boston 1904.

The Little Colonel in Arizona. Boston 1904.

The Quilt that Jack Built; How He Won the Bicycle. Boston 1905 [1904].

In the Desert of Waiting. Boston 1905.

The Little Colonel's Christmas Vacation. Boston [1905].

Keeping Tryst; a Tale of King Arthur's Time. Boston 1906.

The Little Colonel: Maid of Honor. Boston 1906.

Mildred's Inheritance. Boston 1906.

Legend of the Bleeding Heart. Boston 1907.

The Little Colonel's Knight Comes Riding. Boston 1907.

Mary Ware. Boston 1908.

The Rescue of the Princess Winsome; a Fairy Play for Old and Young. Boston 1908.

The Jester's Sword. Boston 1909.

The Little Colonel Good Times Book. Boston 1909.

The Three Weavers. Boston 1909.

The Little Colonel Doll Book. Boston 1910.

Mary Ware in Texas. Boston 1910.

Travellers Five, Along Life's Highway. Boston 1911.

JOHNSTON BIBLIOGRAPHY

Mary Ware's Promised Land. Boston 1912.

Miss Santa Claus of the Pullman. New York 1913.

Georgina of the Rainbows. New York 1916.

Georgina's Service Stars. New York 1918.

The Little Man in Motley. Boston 1918.

Story of the Red Cross as Told to the Little Colonel. Boston 1918.

It Was the Road to Jericho. New York 1919.

The Road of the Loving Heart. Boston 1922.

For Pierre's Sake and Other Stories. Boston [c. 1934].

Selected References:

Vandercook, Margaret W. "Annie Fellows Johnston, the Beloved Writer of Books for Young Folk." *St. Nicholas,* December 1913.

Johnston, Annie Fellows. *The Land of the Little Colonel: Reminiscence and Autobiography.* Boston 1929.

TWO LITTLE CONFEDERATES

THE OLD MAN WALKED UP TO THE DOOR, AND STANDING ON ONE SIDE FLUNG IT OPEN.

TWO LITTLE CONFEDERATES

BY

THOMAS NELSON PAGE

ILLUSTRATED

NEW YORK
CHARLES SCRIBNER'S SONS
1888

Press of J. J. Little & Co.
Astor Place, New York.

TO MY MOTHER

LIST OF ILLUSTRATIONS.

TWO LITTLE CONFEDERATES.

CHAPTER I.

THE "Two Little Confederates" lived at Oakland. It was not a handsome place, as modern ideas go, but down in Old Virginia, where the standard was different from the later one, it passed in old times as one of the best plantations in all that region. The boys thought it the greatest place in the world, of course excepting Richmond, where they had been one year to the fair, and had seen a man pull fire out of his mouth, and do other wonderful things. It was quite secluded. It lay, it is true, right between two of the county roads, the Court-house Road being on one side, and on the other the great "Mountain Road," down which the large covered wagons with six horses and jingling bells used to go; but the lodge lay this side of the one, and "the big woods," where the boys shot squirrels, and hunted 'possums and coons, and which reached to the edge of "Holetown," stretched between the house and the other, so that the big gate-post where the semi-weekly mail was left by the mail-rider each Tuesday and Friday afternoon was a long walk, even by the near cut through the woods. The railroad was ten miles away by the road. There was a nearer way, only about half the distance, by which the negroes used to walk, and which during the war, after all the horses were gone, the boys, too, learned to travel; but before that, the road by Trinity Church and Honeyman's Bridge was the only route, and the other was simply a dim bridle-path, and the "horseshoe-ford" was known to the initiated alone.

The mansion itself was known on the plantation as "the great-house," to distinguish it from all the other houses on the place, of which there were many. It had as many wings as the angels in the vision of Ezekiel.

These additions had been made, some in one generation, some in another, as the size of the family required; and finally, when there was no side of the original structure to which another wing could be joined, a separate building had been erected on the edge of the yard which was called "The Office," and was used as such, as well as for a lodging-place by the young men of the family. The privilege of sleeping in the Office was highly esteemed, for, like the *toga virilis*, it marked the entrance upon manhood of the youths who were fortunate enough to enjoy it. There smoking was admissible, there the guns were kept in the corner, and there the dogs were allowed to sleep at the feet of their young masters, or in bed with them, if they preferred it.

In one of the rooms in this building the boys went to school whilst small, and another they looked forward to having as their own when they should be old enough to be elevated to the coveted dignity of sleeping in the Office. Hugh already slept there, and gave himself airs in proportion; but Hugh they regarded as a very aged person; not as old, it was true, as their cousins who came down from college at Christmas, and who, at the first outbreak of war, all rushed into the army; but each of these was in the boys' eyes a Methuselah. Hugh had his own horse and the double-barrelled gun, and when a fellow got those there was little material difference between him and other men, even if he did have to go to the academy,—which was really something like going to school.

The boys were Frank and Willy; Frank being the eldest. They went by several names on the place. Their mother called them her "little men," with much pride; Uncle Balla spoke of them as "them chillern," which generally implied something of reproach; and Lucy Ann, who had been taken into the house to "run after" them when they were little boys, always coupled their names as "Frank 'n' Willy." Peter and Cole did the same when their mistress was not by.

When there first began to be talk at Oakland about the war, the boys thought it would be a dreadful thing; their principal ideas about war being formed from an intimate acquaintance with the Bible and its accounts of the wars of the Children of Israel, in which men, women and children were invariably put to the sword. This gave a vivid conception of its horrors.

One evening, in the midst of a discussion about the approaching crisis, Willy astonished the company, who were discussing the merits of probable leaders of the Union armies, by suddenly announcing that he'd "bet they did n't have any general who could beat Joab."

Up to the time of the war, the boys had led a very uneventful, but a very pleasant life. They used to go hunting with Hugh, their older brother, when he would let them go, and after the cows with Peter and Cole. Old Balla, the driver, was their boon comrade and adviser, and taught them to make whips, and traps for hares and birds, as he had taught them to ride and to cobble shoes.

He lived alone (for his wife had been set free years before, and lived in Philadelphia). His room over "the old kitchen" was the boys' play-room when he would permit them to come in. There were so many odds and ends in it that it was a delightful place.

Then the boys played blindman's-buff in the house, or hide-and-seek about the yard or garden, or upstairs in their den, a narrow alcove at the top of the house.

The little willow-shadowed creek, that ran through the meadow behind the barn, was one of their haunts. They fished in it for minnows and little perch; they made dams and bathed in it; and sometimes they played pirates upon its waters.

Once they made an extended search up and down its banks for any fragments of Pharaoh's chariots which might have been washed up so high; but that was when they were younger and did not have much sense.

CHAPTER II.

THERE was great excitement at Oakland during the John Brown raid, and the boys' grandmother used to pray for him and Cook, whose pictures were in the papers.

The boys became soldiers, and drilled punctiliously with guns which they got Uncle Balla to make for them. Frank was the captain, Willy the first lieutenant, and a dozen or more little negroes composed the rank and file, Peter and Cole being trusted file-closers.

A little later they found their sympathies all on the side of peace and the preservation of the Union. Their uncle was for keeping the Union unbroken, and ran for the Convention against Colonel Richards, who was the chief officer of the militia in the county, and was as blood-thirsty as Tamerlane, who reared the pyramid of skulls, and as hungry for military renown as the great Napoleon, about whom the boys had read.

There was immense excitement in the county over the election. Though the boys' mother had made them add to their prayers a petition that their Uncle William might win, and that he might secure the blessings of peace; and, though at family prayers, night and morning, the same petition was presented, the boys' uncle was beaten at the polls by a large majority. And then they knew there was bound to be war, and that it must be very wicked. They almost felt the "invader's heel," and the invaders were invariably spoken of as "cruel," and the heel was described as of "iron," and was always mentioned as engaged in the act of crushing. They would have been terribly alarmed at this cruel invasion had they not been reassured by the general belief of the community that one Southerner could whip ten Yankees, and that, collectively, the South could drive back the North with pop-guns. When the war actually broke out, the boys were the most enthusiastic of rebels, and the troops in Camp Lee did not drill more continuously nor industriously.

Their father, who had been a Whig and opposed secession until the very last, on Virginia's seceding, finally cast his lot with his people, and joined an infantry company; and Uncle William raised and equipped an artillery company, of which he was chosen captain; but the infantry was too tame and the artillery too ponderous to suit the boys.

They were taken to see the drill of the county troop of cavalry, with its prancing horses and clanging sabres. It was commanded by a cousin; and from that moment they were cavalrymen to the core. They flung away their stick-guns in disgust; and Uncle Balla spent two grumbling days fashioning them a stableful of horses with real heads and "sure 'nough" leather bridles.

Once, indeed, a secret attempt was made to utilize the horses and mules which were running in the back pasture; but a premature discovery of the matter ended in such disaster to all concerned that the plan was abandoned, and the boys had to content themselves with their wooden steeds.

The day that the final orders came for their father and uncle to go to Richmond,—from which point they were ordered to "the Peninsula,"—the boys could not understand why every one was suddenly plunged into such distress. Then, next morning, when the soldiers left, the boys could not altogether comprehend it. They thought it was a very fine thing to be allowed to ride Frank and Hun, the two war-horses, with their new, deep army saddles and long bits. They cried when their father and uncle said good-bye, and went away; but it was because their mother looked so pale and ill, and not because they did not think it was all grand. They had no doubt that all would come back soon, for old Uncle Billy, the "head-man," who had been born down in "Little York," where Cornwallis surrendered, had expressed the sentiment of the whole plantation when he declared, as he sat in the back yard surrounded by an admiring throng, and surveyed with pride the two glittering sabres which he had allowed no one but himself to polish, that "Ef them Britishers jest sees dese swodes dee'll run!" The boys tried to explain to him that these were not British, but Yankees,—but he was hard to convince. Even Lucy Ann, who was incurably afraid of everything like a gun or fire-arm, partook of the general fervor, and boasted effusively that she had actually "tetched Marse John's big pistils."

Hugh, who was fifteen, and was permitted to accompany

his father to Richmond, was regarded by the boys with a feeling of mingled envy and veneration, which he accepted with dignified complacency.

Frank and Willy soon found that war brought some immunities. The house filled up so with the families of cousins and friends who were refugees that the boys were obliged to sleep in the Office, and thus they felt that, at a bound, they were almost as old as Hugh.

There were the cousins from Gloucester, from the Valley, and families of relatives from Baltimore and New York, who had come south on the declaration of war. Their favorite was their Cousin Belle, whose beauty at once captivated both boys. This was the first time that the boys knew anything of girls, except their own sister, Evelyn; and after a brief period, during which the novelty gave them pleasure, the inability of the girls to hunt, climb trees, or play knucks, etc., and the additional restraint which their presence imposed, caused them to hold the opinion that "girls were no good."

CHAPTER III.

IN course of time they saw a great deal of "the army,"—which meant the Confederates. The idea that the Yankees could ever get to Oakland never entered any one's head. It was understood that the army lay between Oakland and them and surely they could never get by the innumerable soldiers who were always passing up one road or the other, and who, day after day and night after night, were coming to be fed, and were rapidly eating up everything that had been left on the place. By the end of the first year they had been coming so long that they made scarcely any difference; but the first time a regiment camped in the neighborhood it created great excitement.

It became known one night that a cavalry regiment, in which were several of their cousins, was encamped at Honeyman's Bridge, and the boys' mother determined to send a supply of provisions for the camp next morning; so several sheep were killed, the smoke-house was opened, and all night long the great fires in the kitchen and wash-house glowed; and even then there was not room, so that a big fire was kindled in the back yard, beside which saddles of mutton were roasted in the tin kitchens. Everybody was ' rushing."

The boys were told that they might go to see the soldiers, and as they had to get off long before daylight, they went to bed early, and left all "the other boys"—that is, Peter and Cole and other colored children—squatting about the fires and trying to help the cooks to pile on wood.

It was hard to leave the exciting scene.

They were very sleepy the next morning; indeed, they seemed scarcely to have fallen asleep when Lucy Ann shook them; but they jumped up without the usual application of cold water in their faces, which Lucy Ann so delighted to make; and in a little while they were out in the yard, where Balla was standing holding three horses,—their mother's riding-horse; another with a side-saddle for their Cousin Belle, whose brother was in the regiment; and one for himself,—and Peter and Cole were holding the carriage-horses for the boys, and several other men were holding mules.

Great hampers covered with white napkins were on the porch, and the savory smell decided the boys not to eat their breakfast, but to wait and take their share with the soldiers.

The roads were so bad that the carriage could not go; and as the boys' mother wished to get the provisions to the soldiers before they broke camp, they had to set out at once. In a few minutes they were all in the saddle, the boys and their mother and Cousin Belle in front, and Balla and the other servants following close behind, each holding before him a hamper, which looked queer and shadowy as they rode on in the darkness.

The sky, which was filled with stars when they set out,

grew white as they splashed along mile after mile through the mud. Then the road became clearer; they could see into the woods, and the sky changed to a rich pink, like the color of peach-blossoms. Their horses were covered with mud up to the saddle-skirts. They turned into a lane only half a mile from the bridge, and, suddenly, a bugle rang out down in the wooded bottom below them, and the boys hardly could be kept from putting their horses to a run, so fearful were they that the soldiers were leaving, and that they should not see them. Their mother, however, told them that this was probably the reveille, or "rising-bell," of the soldiers. She rode on at a good sharp canter, and the boys were diverting themselves over a discussion as to who would act the part of Lucy Ann in waking the regiment of soldiers, when they turned a curve, and at the end of the road, a few hundred yards ahead, stood several horsemen.

"There they are," exclaimed both boys.

"No, that is a picket," said their mother; "gallop on, Frank, and tell them we are bringing breakfast for the regiment."

Frank dashed ahead, and soon they saw a soldier ride forward to meet him, and, after a few words, return with him to his comrades. Then, while they were still a hundred yards distant, they saw Frank, who had received some directions, start off again toward the bridge, at a hard gallop. The picket had told him to go straight on down the hill, and he would find the camp just the other side of the bridge.

He accordingly rode on, feeling very important at being allowed to go alone to the camp on such a mission.

As he reached a turn in the road, just above the river, the whole regiment lay swarming below him among the large trees on the bank of the little stream. The horses were picketed to bushes and stakes, in long rows, the saddles lying on the ground, not far off; and hundreds of men were moving about, some in full uniform and others without coat or vest. A half-dozen wagons with sheets on them stood on one side among the trees, near which several fires were smoking, with men around them.

As Frank clattered up to the bridge, a soldier with a gun on his arm, who had been standing by the railing, walked out to the middle of the bridge.

"Halt! Where are you going in such a hurry, my young man?" he said.

"I wish to see the colonel," said Frank, repeating as nearly as he could the words the picket had told him.

"What do you want with him?"

Frank was tempted not to tell him; but he was so impatient to deliver his message before the others should arrive, that he told him what he had come for.

"There he is," said the sentinel, pointing to a place among the trees where stood at least five hundred men.

Frank looked, expecting to recognize the colonel by his noble bearing, or splendid uniform, or some striking marks.

"Where?" he asked, in doubt; for while a number of the men were in uniform, he knew these to be privates.

"There," said the sentry, pointing; "by that stump, near the yellow horse-blanket."

Frank looked again. The only man he could fix upon by the description was a young fellow, washing his face in a tin basin, and he felt that this could not be the colonel; but he did not like to appear dull, so he thanked the man and rode on, thinking he would go to the point indicated, and ask some one else to show him the officer.

He felt quite grand as he rode in among the men, who, he thought, would recognize his importance and treat him accordingly; but, as he passed on, instead of paying him the respect he had expected, they began to guy him with all sorts of questions.

"Hullo, bud, going to jine the cavalry?" asked one. "Which is oldest; you or your horse?" inquired another.

"How's pa—and ma?" "Does your mother know you 're out?" asked others. One soldier walked up, and putting his hand on the bridle, proceeded affably to ask him after his health, and that of every member of his family. At first Frank did not understand that they were making fun of him, but it dawned on him when the man asked him solemnly:

"Are there any Yankees around, that you were running away so fast just now?"

"No; if there were I'd never have found *you* here," said

Frank, shortly, in reply; which at once turned the tide in his favor and diverted the ridicule from himself to his teaser, who was seized by some of his comrades and carried off with much laughter and slapping on the back.

"I wish to see Colonel Marshall," said Frank, pushing his way through the group that surrounded him, and riding up to the man who was still occupied at the basin on the stump.

"All right, sir, I'm the man," said the individual, cheerily looking up with his face dripping and rosy from its recent scrubbing.

"You the colonel!" exclaimed Frank, suspicious that he was again being ridiculed, and thinking it impossible that this slim, rosy-faced youngster, who was scarcely stouter than Hugh, and who was washing in a tin basin, could be the commander of all these soldierly-looking men, many of whom were old enough to be his father.

"Yes, I'm the lieutenant-colonel. I'm in command," said the gentleman, smiling at him over the towel.

Something made Frank understand that this was really the officer, and he gave his message, which was received with many expressions of thanks.

"Won't you get down? Here, Campbell, take this horse, will you?" he called to a soldier, as Frank sprang from his horse. The orderly stepped forward and took the bridle.

"Now, come with me," said the colonel, leading the way. "We must get ready to receive your mother. There are

"I'M IN COMMAND" SAID THE GENTLEMAN, SMILING AT HIM OVER THE TOWEL.

some ladies coming—and breakfast," he called to a group who were engaged in the same occupation he had just ended, and whom Frank knew by instinct to be officers.

The information seemed to electrify the little knot addressed; for they began to rush around, and in a few moments they all were in their uniforms, and surrounding the colonel, who, having brushed his hair with the aid of a little glass hung on a bush, had hurried into his coat and was buckling on his sword and giving orders in a way which at once satisfied Frank that he was every inch a colonel.

"Now let us go and receive your mother," said he to the boy. As he strode through the camp with his coat tightly buttoned, his soft hat set jauntily on the side of his head, his plumes sweeping over its side, and his sword clattering at his spurred heel, he presented a very different appearance from that which he had made a little before, with his head in a tin basin, and his face covered with lather. In fact, Colonel Marshall was already a noted officer, and before the end of the war he attained still higher rank and reputation.

The colonel met the rest of the party at the bridge, and introduced himself and several officers who soon joined him. The negroes were directed to take the provisions over to the other side of the stream into the camp, and in a little while the whole regiment were enjoying the breakfast. The boys and their mother had at the colonel's request joined his mess, in which was one of their cousins, the brother of their cousin Belle.

2

The gentlemen could eat scarcely anything, they were so busy attending to the wants of the ladies. The colonel, particularly, waited on their cousin Belle all the time.

As soon as they had finished the colonel left them, and a bugle blew. In a minute all was bustle. Officers were giving orders ; horses were saddled and brought out ; and, by what seemed magic to the boys, the men, who just before were scattered about among the trees laughing and eating, were standing by their horses all in proper order. The colonel and the officers came and said good-bye.

Again the bugle blew. Every man was in his saddle. A few words by the colonel, followed by other words from the captains, and the column started, turning across the bridge, the feet of the horses thundering on the planks. Then the regiment wound up the hill at a walk, the men singing snatches of a dozen songs, of which "The Bonnie Blue Flag," "Lorena," and "Carry me Back to Old Virginia Shore," were the chief ones.

It seemed to the boys that to be a soldier was the noblest thing on earth ; and that this regiment could do anything.

CHAPTER IV.

AFTER this it became a common thing for passing regiments to camp near Oakland, and the fire blazed many a night, cooking for the soldiers, till the chickens were crowing in the morning. The negroes all had hen-houses and raised their own chickens, and when a camp was near them they used to drive a thriving trade on their own account, selling eggs and chickens to the privates while the officers were entertained in the "gret house."

It was thought an honor to furnish food to the soldiers. Every soldier was to the boys a hero, and each young officer might rival Ivanhoe or Cœur de Lion.

It was not a great while, however, before they learned that all soldiers were not like their favorite knights. At any rate, thefts were frequent. The absence of men from the plantations, and the constant passing of strangers made stealing easy; hen-roosts were robbed time after time, and even pigs and sheep were taken without any trace of the thieves. The boys' hen-house, however, which was in the yard, had never been troubled. It was about their only possession, and they took great pride in it.

One night the boys were fast asleep in their room in the office, with old Bruno and Nick curled up on their sheepskins on the floor. Hugh was away, so the boys were the only "men" on the place, and felt that they were the protectors of the plantation. The frequent thefts had made every one very suspicious, and the boys had made up their minds to be on the watch, and, if possible, to catch the thief.

The negroes said that the deserters did the stealing.

On the night in question, the boys were sound asleep when old Bruno gave a low growl, and then began walking and sniffing up and down the room. Soon Nick gave a sharp, quick bark.

Frank waked first. He was not startled, for the dogs were in the habit of barking whenever they wished to go out-of-doors. Now, however, they kept it up, and it was in a strain somewhat different from their usual signal.

"What's the matter with you? Go and lie down, Bruno," called Frank. "Hush up, Nick!" But Bruno would not lie down, and Nick would not keep quiet, though at the sound of Frank's voice they felt less responsibility, and contented themselves with a low growling.

After a little while Frank was on the point of dropping off to sleep again, when he heard a sound out in the yard, which at once thoroughly awakened him. He nudged Willy in the side.

"Willy—Willy, wake up; there's some one moving around outdoors."

"Umm-mm," groaned Willy, turning over and settling himself for another nap.

The sound of a chicken chirping out in fright reached Frank's ear.

"Wake up, Willy!" he called, pinching him hard. "There's some one at the hen-house."

Willy was awake in a second. The boys consulted as to what should be done. Willy was sceptical. He thought Frank had been dreaming, or that it was only Uncle Balla, or "some one" moving about the yard. But a second cackle of warning reached them, and in a minute both boys were out of bed pulling on their clothes with trembling impatience.

"Let's go and wake Uncle Balla," proposed Willy, getting himself all tangled in the legs of his trousers.

"No; I'll tell you what, let's catch him ourselves," suggested Frank.

"All right," assented Willy. "We'll catch him and lock him up; suppose he's got a pistol? your gun maybe won't go off; it does n't always burst the cap."

"Well, your old musket is loaded, and you can hold him, while I snap the cap at him, and get it ready."

"All right—I can't find my jacket—I'll hold him."

"Where in the world is my hat?" whispered Frank. "Never mind, it must be in the house. Let's go out the back way. We can get out without his hearing us."

"What shall we do with the dogs? Let's shut them up."

"No, let's take 'em with us. We can keep them quiet and hold 'em in, and they can track him if he gets away."

"All right;" and the boys slowly opened the door, and

crept stealthily out, Frank clutching his double-barrelled gun, and Willy hugging a heavy musket which he had found and claimed as one of the prizes of war. It was almost pitch-dark.

They decided that one should take one side of the hen-house, and one the other side (in such a way that if they had to shoot, they would almost certainly shoot one another!) but before they had separated both dogs jerked loose from their hands and dashed away in the darkness, barking furiously.

"There he goes round the garden," shouted Willy, as the sound of footsteps like those of a man running with all his might came from the direction which the dogs had taken.

"Come on," and both started; but, after taking a few steps, they stopped to listen so that they might trace the fugitive.

A faint noise behind them arrested their attention, and Frank tiptoed back toward the hen-house. It was too dark to see much, but he heard the hen-house door creak, and was conscious even in the darkness that it was being pushed slowly open.

"Here's one, Willy," he shouted, at the same time putting his gun to his shoulder and pulling the trigger. The hammer fell with a sharp "click" just as the door was snatched to with a bang. The cap had failed to explode, or the chicken-eating days of the individual in the hen-house would have ended then and there.

The boys stood for some moments with their guns pointed at the door of the hen-house expecting the person within to attempt to burst out; but the click of the hammer and their hurried conference without, in which it was promptly agreed to let him have both barrels if he appeared, reconciled him to remaining within.

After some time it was decided to go and wake Uncle Balla, and confer with him as to the proper disposition of their captive. Accordingly, Frank went off to obtain help, while Willy remained to watch the hen-house. As Frank left he called back:

"Willy, you take good aim at him, and if he pokes his head out—let him have it!"

This Willy solemnly promised to do.

Frank was hardly out of hearing before Willy was surprised to hear the prisoner call him by name in the most friendly and familiar manner, although the voice was a strange one.

"Willy, is that you?" called the person inside.

"Yes."

"Where's Frank?"

"Gone to get Uncle Balla."

"Did you see that other fellow?"

"Yes."

"I wish you 'd shot him. He brought me here and played a joke on me. He told me this was a house I could sleep in, and shut me up in here,—and blest if I don't b'lieve it's nothin' but a hen-house. Let me out here a minute," he continued, after a pause, cajolingly.

"No, I won't," said Willy firmly, getting his gun ready

There was a pause, and then from the depths of the hen-house issued the most awful groan:

"Umm! Ummm!! Ummmm!!!"

Willy was frightened.

"Umm! Umm!" was repeated.

"What's the matter with you?" asked Willy, feeling sorry in spite of himself.

"Oh! Oh! Oh! I'm so sick," groaned the man in the hen-house.

"How? What's the matter?"

"That man that fooled me in here gave me something to drink, and it's pizened me; oh! oh! oh! I'm dying."

It was a horrible groan.

Willy's heart relented. He moved to the door and was just about to open it to look in when a light flashed across the yard from Uncle Balla's house, and he saw him coming with a flaming light-wood knot in his hand.

CHAPTER V.

INSTEAD of opening the door, therefore, Willy called to the old man, who was leisurely crossing the yard:

"Run, Uncle Balla. Quick, run!"

At the call Old Balla and Frank set out as fast as they could.

"What's the matter? Is he done kill de chickens? Is he done got away?" the old man asked, breathlessly.

"No, he 's dyin'," shouted Willy.

"Hi! is you shoot him?" asked the old driver.

"No, that other man 's poisoned him. He was the robber and he fooled this one," explained Willy, opening the door and peeping anxiously in.

"Go 'long, boy,—now, d' ye ever heah de better o' dat?—dat man 's foolin' wid you; jes' tryin' to git yo' to let him out."

"No, he is n't," said Willy; "you ought to have heard him."

But both Balla and Frank were laughing at him, so he felt very shamefaced. He was relieved by hearing another groan.

"Oh, oh, oh! Ah, ah!"

"You hear that?" he asked, triumphantly.

"I boun' I 'll see what 's the matter with him, the roscol! Stan' right dyah, y' all, an' if he try to run shoot him, but mine you don' hit *me*," and the old man walked up to the door, and standing on one side flung it open. "What you doin' in dyah after dese chillern's chickens?" he called fiercely.

"Hello, old man, 's 'at you? I 's mighty sick," muttered the person within. Old Balla held his torch inside the house, amid a confused cackle and flutter of fowls.

"Well, ef 't ain' a white man, and a soldier at dat!" he exclaimed. "What you doin' heah, robbin' white folks' hen-roos'?" he called, roughly. "Git up off dat groun'; you ain' sick."

"Let me get up, Sergeant,—hic—don't you heah the roll-call?—the tent 's mighty dark; what you fool me in here for?" muttered the man inside.

The boys could see that he was stretched out on the floor, apparently asleep, and that he was a soldier in uniform. Balla stepped inside.

"Is he dead?" asked both boys as Balla caught him by the arms, lifted him, and let him fall again limp on the floor.

"Nor, he 's dead-drunk," said Balla, picking up an empty flask. "Come on out. Let me see what I gwi' do wid you?" he said, scratching his head.

"I know what I gwi' do wid you. I gwi' lock you up right whar you is."

"Uncle Balla, s'pose he gets well, won't he get out?"

"Ain' *I* gwi' lock him up? Dat 's good from you, who was jes' gwi' let 'im out ef me an' Frank had n't come up when we did."

Willy stepped back abashed. His heart accused him and told him the charge was true. Still he ventured one more question:

"Had n't you better take the hens out?"

"Nor; 't ain' no use to teck nuttin' out dyah. Ef he comes to, he know we got im, an' he dyahson' trouble nuttin'."

And the old man pushed to the door and fastened the iron hasp over the strong staple. Then, as the lock had been broken, he took a large nail from his pocket and fastened it in the staple with a stout string so that it could not be shaken out. All the time he was working he was talking to the boys, or rather to himself, for their benefit.

"Now, you see ef we don' find him heah in the mornin'! Willy jes' gwi' let you get 'way, but a *man* got you now, wha'ar' been handlin' horses an' know how to hole 'em in the stalls. I boun' he 'll have to butt like a ram to git out dis log hen-house," he said, finally, as he finished tying the last knot in his string, and gave the door a vigorous rattle to test its strength.

Willy had been too much abashed at his mistake to fully appreciate all of the witticisms over the prisoner, but Frank enjoyed them almost as much as Unc' Balla himself.

"Now y' all go 'long to bed, an' I 'll go back an' teck

a little nap myself," said he, in parting. "Ef he gits out that hen-house I 'll give you ev'y chicken I got. But he ain' *gwine* git out. A *man's* done fasten him up dyah."

The boys went off to bed, Willy still feeling depressed over his ridiculous mistake. They were soon fast asleep, and if the dogs barked again they did not hear them.

The next thing they knew, Lucy Ann, convulsed with laughter, was telling them a story about Uncle Balla and the man in the hen-house. They jumped up, and pulling on their clothes ran out in the yard, thinking to see the prisoner.

Instead of doing so, they found Uncle Balla standing by the hen-house with a comical look of mystification and chagrin; the roof had been lifted off at one end and not only the prisoner, but every chicken was gone!

The boys were half inclined to cry; Balla's look, however, set them to laughing.

"Unc' Balla, you got to give me every chicken you got, 'cause you said you would," said Willy.

"Go 'way from heah, boy. Don' pester me when I studyin' to see which way he got out."

"You ain't never had a horse get through the roof before, have you?" said Frank.

"Go 'way from here, I tell you," said the old man, walking around the house, looking at it.

As the boys went back to wash and dress themselves, they heard Balla explaining to Lucy Ann and some of the other servants that "the man them chillern let git away had just come back and tooken out the one he had locked up"; a solution of the mystery he always stoutly insisted upon.

One thing, however, the person's escape effected—it prevented Willy's ever hearing any more of his mistake; but that did not keep him now and then from asking Uncle Balla "if he had fastened his horses well."

CHAPTER VI.

THESE hens were not the last things stolen from Oakland. Nearly all the men in the country had gone with the army. Indeed, with the exception of a few overseers who remained to work the farms, every man in the neighborhood, between the ages of seventeen and fifty, was in the army. The country was thus left almost wholly unprotected, and it would have been entirely so but for the "Home Guard," as it was called, which was a company composed of young boys and the few old men who remained at home, and who had volunteered for service as a local guard, or police body, for the neighborhood of their homes.

Occasionally, too, later on, a small detachment of men, under a leader known as a "conscript-officer," would come through the country hunting for any men who were subject to the conscript law but who had evaded it, and for deserters who had run away from the army and refused to return.

These two classes of troops, however, stood on a very different footing. The Home Guard was regarded with much respect, for it was composed of those whose extreme age or youth alone withheld them from active service; and every youngster in its ranks looked upon it as a training school, and was ready to die in defence of his home if need were, and, besides, expected to obtain permission to go into the army "next year."

The conscript-guard, on the other hand, were grown men, and were thought to be shirking the very dangers and hardships into which they were trying to force others.

A few miles from Oakland, on the side toward the mountain road and beyond the big woods, lay a district of virgin forest and old-field pines which, even before the war, had acquired a reputation of an unsavory nature, though its inhabitants were a harmless people. No highways ran through this region, and the only roads which entered it were mere wood-ways, filled with bushes and carpeted with pine-tags; and, being travelled only by the inhabitants, appeared to outsiders "to jes' peter out," as the phrase went. This territory was known by the unpromising name of Holetown.

Its denizens were a peculiar but kindly race known to the boys as "poor white folks," and called by the negroes, with great contempt, "po' white trash." Some of them owned small places in the pines; but the majority were simply tenants. They were an inoffensive people, and their worst vices were intemperance and evasion of the tax-laws.

They made their living—or rather, they existed—by fishing and hunting; and, to eke it out, attempted the cultivation of little patches of corn and tobacco near their cabins, or in the bottoms where small branches ran into the stream already mentioned.

In appearance they were usually so thin and sallow that

one had to look at them twice to see them clearly. At best, they looked vague and illusive.

They were brave enough. At the outbreak of the war nearly all of the men in this community enlisted, thinking, as many others did, that war was more like play than work, and consisted more of resting than of laboring. Although most of them, when in battle, showed the greatest fearlessness, yet the duties of camp soon became irksome to them, and they grew sick of the restraint and drilling of camp-life; so some of them, when refused a furlough, took it, and came home. Others stayed at home after leave had ended, feeling secure in their stretches of pine and swamp, not only from the feeble efforts of the conscript-guard, but from any parties who might be sent in search of them.

In this way it happened, as time went by, that Hole-town became known to harbor a number of deserters.

According to the negroes, it was full of them; and many stories were told about glimpses of men dodging behind trees in the big woods, or rushing away through the underbrush like wild cattle. And, though the grown people doubted whether the negroes had not been startled by some of the hogs, which were quite wild, feeding in the woods, the boys were satisfied that the negroes really had seen deserters.

This became a certainty when there came report after report of these wood-skulkers, and when the conscript-guard, with the brightest of uniforms, rode by with as much show and noise as if on a fox-hunt. Then it became known that deserters were, indeed, infesting the piny district of Holetown, and in considerable numbers.

Some of them, it was said, were pursuing agriculture and all their ordinary vocations as openly as in time of peace, and more industriously. They had a regular code of signals, and nearly every person in the Holetown settlement was in league with them.

When the conscript-guard came along, there would be a rush of tow-headed children through the woods, or some of the women about the cabins would blow a horn lustily; after which not a man could be found in all the district. The horn told just how many men were in the guard, and which path they were following; every member of the troop being honored with a short, quick "toot."

"What are you blowing that horn for?" sternly asked the guard one morning of an old woman,—old Mrs. Hall, who stood out in front of her little house blowing like Boreas in the pictures.

"Jes' blowin' fur Millindy to come to dinner," she said, sullenly. "Can't y' all let a po' 'ooman call her gals to git some 'n' to eat? You got all her boys in d'army, killin' 'em; why n't yo' go and git kilt some yo'self, 'stidder ridin' 'bout heah tromplin' all over po' folk's chickens?"

When the troop returned in the evening, she was still blowing; "blowin' fur Millindy to come home," she said, with more sharpness than before. But there must have been many Millindys, for horns were sounding all through the settlement.

The deserters, at such times, were said to take to the swamps, and marvellous rumors were abroad of one or more caves, all fitted up, wherein they concealed themselves, like the robbers in the stories the boys were so fond of reading.

After a while thefts of pigs and sheep became so common that they were charged to the deserters.

Finally it grew to be such a pest that the ladies in the neighborhood asked the Home Guard to take action in the matter, and after some delay it became known that this valorous body was going to invade Holetown and capture the deserters or drive them away. Hugh was to accompany them, of course; and he looked very handsome, as well as very important, when he started out on horseback to join the troop. It was his first active service; and with his trousers in his boots and his pistol in his belt he looked as brave as Julius Cæsar, and quite laughed at his mother's fears for him, as she kissed him good-bye and walked out with him to his horse, which Balla held at the gate.

The boys asked leave to go with him; but Hugh was so scornful over their request, and looked so soldierly as he galloped away with the other men that the boys felt as cheap as possible.

CHAPTER VII.

WHEN the boys went into the house they found that their Aunt Mary had a headache that morning, and, even with the best intentions of doing her duty in teaching them, had been forced to go to bed. Their mother was too much occupied with her charge of providing for a family of over a dozen white persons, and five times as many colored dependents, to give any time to acting as substitute in the school-room, so the boys found themselves with a holiday before them. It seemed vain to try to shoot duck on the creek, and the perch were averse to biting. The boys accordingly determined to take both guns and to set out for a real hunt in the big woods.

They received their mother's permission, and after a lunch was prepared they started in high glee, talking about the squirrels and birds they expected to kill.

Frank had his gun, and Willy had the musket; and both carried a plentiful supply of powder and some tolerably round slugs made from cartridges.

They usually hunted in the part of the woods nearest the house, and they knew that game was not very abundant there; so, as a good long day was before them, they determined to go over to the other side of the woods.

They accordingly pushed on, taking a path which led through the forest. They went entirely through the big woods without seeing anything but one squirrel, and presently found themselves at the extreme edge of Holetown. They were just grumbling at the lack of game when they heard a distant horn. The sound came from perhaps a mile or more away, but was quite distinct.

"What 's that? Somebody fox-hunting?—or is it a dinner-horn?" asked Willy, listening intently.

"It 's a horn to warn deserters, that 's what 't is," said Frank, pleased to show his superior knowledge.

"I tell you what to do:—let 's go and hunt deserters," said Willy, eagerly.

"All right. Won't that be fun!" and both boys set out down the road toward a point where they knew one of the paths ran into the pine-district, talking of the numbers of prisoners they expected to take.

In an instant they were as alert and eager as young hounds on a trail. They had mapped out a plan before, and they knew exactly what they had to do. Frank was the captain, by right of his being older; and Willy was lieutenant, and was to obey orders. The chief thing that troubled them was that they did not wish to be seen by any of the women or children about the cabins, for they all knew the boys, because they were accustomed to come to Oakland for supplies; then, too, the boys wished to remain on friendly terms with their neighbors. Another thing worried them. They did not know what to do with their prisoners after they should have captured them. However, they pushed on and soon came to a dim cart-way, which ran at right-angles to the main road and which went into the very heart of Hole-town. Here they halted to reconnoitre and to inspect their weapons.

Even from the main road, the track, as it led off through the overhanging woods with thick underbrush of chinquapin bushes, appeared to the boys to have something strange about it, though they had at other times walked it from end to end. Still, they entered boldly, clutching their guns. Willy suggested that they should go in Indian file and that the rear one should step in the other's footprints as the Indians do; but Frank thought it was best to walk abreast, as the Indians walked in their peculiar way only to prevent an enemy who crossed their trail from knowing how many they were; and, so far from it being any disadvantage for the deserters to know *their* number, it was even better that they should know there were two, so that they would not attack from the rear. Accordingly, keeping abreast, they struck in; each taking the woods on one side of the road, which he was to watch and for which he was to be responsible.

The farther they went the more indistinct the track became, and the wilder became the surrounding woods. They proceeded with great caution, examining every particularly thick clump of bushes; peeping behind each very large tree; and occasionally even taking a glance up among its boughs;

for they had themselves so often planned how, if pursued, they would climb trees and conceal themselves, that they would not have been at all surprised to find a fierce deserter, armed to the teeth, crouching among the branches.

Though they searched carefully every spot where a deserter could possibly lurk, they passed through the oak woods and were deep in the pines without having seen any foe or heard a noise which could possibly proceed from one. A squirrel had daringly leaped from the trunk of a hickory-tree and run into the woods, right before them, stopping impudently to take a good look at them; but they were hunting larger game than squirrels, and they resisted the temptation to take a shot at him,—an exercise of virtue which brought them a distinct feeling of pleasure. They were, however, beginning to be embarrassed as to their next course. They could hear the dogs barking, farther on in the pines, and knew they were approaching the vicinity of the settlement; for they had crossed the little creek which ran through a thicket of elder bushes and "gums," and which marked the boundary of Holetown. Little paths, too, every now and then turned off from the main track and went into the pines, each leading to a cabin or bit of creek-bottom deeper in. They therefore were in a real dilemma concerning what to do; and Willy's suggestion, to eat lunch, was a welcome one. They determined to go a little way into the woods, where they could not be seen, and had just taken the lunch out of the game-bag and were turning into a by-path, when they met a man who was coming along at a slow, lounging walk, and carrying a long single-barrelled shot-gun across his arm.

When first they heard him, they thought he might be a deserter; but when he came nearer they saw that he was simply a countryman out hunting; for his old game-bag (from which peeped a squirrel's tail) was over his shoulder, and he had no weapon at all, excepting that old squirrel-gun.

"Good morning, sir," said both boys, politely.

"Mornin'! What luck y' all had?" he asked good-naturedly, stopping and putting the butt of his gun on the ground, and resting lazily on it, preparatory to a chat.

"We're not hunting; we're hunting deserters."

"Huntin' deserters!" echoed the man with a smile which broke into a chuckle of amusement as the thought worked its way into his brain. "Ain't you see' none?"

"No," said both boys in a breath, greatly pleased at his friendliness. "Do you know where any are?"

The man scratched his head, seeming to reflect.

"Well, 'pears to me I hearn tell o' some, 'roun' to'des that-a-ways," making a comprehensive sweep of his arm in the direction just opposite to that which the boys were taking. "I seen the conscrip'-guard a little while ago pokin' 'roun' this-a-way; but Lor', that ain' the way to ketch deserters. I knows every foot o' groun' this-a-way, an' ef they was any deserters roun' here I'd be mighty apt to know it."

This announcement was an extinguisher to the boys' hopes. Clearly, they were going in the wrong direction.

"We are just going to eat our lunch," said Frank; "won't you join us?"

Willy added his invitation to his brother's, and their friend politely accepted, suggesting that they should walk back a little way and find a log. This all three did; and in a few minutes they were enjoying the lunch which the boys' mother had provided, while the stranger was telling the boys his views about deserters, which, to say the least, were very original.

"I seen the conscrip'-guard jes' this mornin', ridin' 'round whar they knowd they war n' no deserters, but ole womens and children," he said with his mouth full. "Why n't they go whar they knows deserters *is?*" he asked.

"Where are they? We heard they had a cave down on the river, and we were going there," declared the boys.

"Down on the river?—a cave? Ain' no cave down thar, without it 's below Rockett's mill; fur I 've hunted and fished ev'y foot o' that river up an' down both sides, an' t' ain' a hole thar, big enough to hide a' ole hyah, I ain' know."

This proof was too conclusive to admit of further argument.

"Why don't *you* go in the army?" asked Willy, after a brief reflection.

"What? Why don't *I* go in the army?" repeated the hunter. "Why, I's *in* the army! You did n' think I war n't in the army, did you?"

The hunter's tone and the expression of his face were so

full of surprise that Willy felt deeply mortified at his rudeness, and began at once to stammer something to explain himself.

"I b'longs to Colonel Marshall's regiment," continued the man, "an' I 's been home sick on leave o' absence. Got wounded in the leg, an' I 's jes' gettin' well. I ain' rightly well enough to go back now, but I 's anxious to git back; I 'm gwine to-morrow mornin' ef I don' go this evenin'. You see I kin hardly walk now!" and to demonstrate his lameness, he got up and limped a few yards. "I ain' well yit," he pursued, returning and dropping into his seat on the log, with his face drawn up by the pain the exertion had brought on.

"Let me see your wound. Is it sore now?" asked Willy, moving nearer to the man with a look expressive of mingled curiosity and sympathy.

"You can't see it; it 's up heah," said the soldier, touching the upper part of his hip; "an' I got another one heah," he added, placing his hand very gently to his side. "This one's whar a Yankee run me through with his sword. Now, that one was where a piece of shell hit me,—I don't keer nothin' 'bout that," and he opened his shirt and showed a triangular, purple scar on his shoulder.

"You certainly must be a brave soldier," exclaimed both boys, impressed at sight of the scar, their voices softened by fervent admiration.

"Yes, I kep' up with the bes' of 'em," he said, with a pleased smile.

Suddenly a horn began to blow, "toot—toot—toot," as if all the "Millindys" in the world were being summoned. It was so near the boys that it quite startled them.

"That 's for the deserters, now," they both exclaimed.

Their friend looked calmly up and down the road, both ways.

"Them rascally conscrip'-guard been tellin' you all that, to gi' 'em some excuse for keepin' out o' th' army theyselves—that 's all. Th' ain' gwine ketch no deserters any whar in all these parts, an' you kin tell 'em so. I 'm gwine down thar an' see what that horn 's a-blown' fur; hit 's somebody's dinner horn, or somp'n'," he added, rising and taking up his game-bag.

"Can't we go with you?" asked the boys.

"Well, nor, I reckon you better not," he drawled; "thar 's some right bad dogs down thar in the pines,—mons'us bad; an' I 's gwine cut through the woods an' see ef I can't pick up a squ'rr'l, gwine 'long, for the ole 'ooman's supper, as I got to go 'way to-night or to-morrow; she 's mighty poorly."

"Is she poorly much?" asked Willy, greatly concerned. "We 'll get mamma to come and see her to-morrow, and bring her some bread."

"Nor, she ain' so sick; that is to say, she jis' poorly and 'sturbed in her mind. She gittin' sort o' old. Here, y' all take these squ'rr'ls," he said, taking the squirrels from his old game-bag and tossing them at Willy's feet. Both boys protested, but he insisted. "Oh, yes; I kin get some mo' fur her."

"Y' all better go home. Well, good-by, much obliged to you," and he strolled off with his gun in the bend of his arm, leaving the boys to admire and talk over his courage.

They turned back, and had gone about a quarter of a mile, when they heard a great trampling of horses behind them. They stopped to listen, and in a little while a squadron of cavalry came in sight. The boys stepped to one side of the road to wait for them, eager to tell the important information they had received from their friend, that there were no deserters in that section. In a hurried consultation they agreed not to tell that they had been hunting deserters themselves, as they knew the soldiers would only have a laugh at their expense.

"Hello, boys, what luck?" called the officer in the lead, in a friendly manner.

They told him they had not shot anything; that the squirrels had been given to them; and then both boys inquired:

"You all hunting for deserters?"

"You seen any?" asked the leader, carelessly, while one or two men pressed their horses forward eagerly.

"No, th' ain't any deserters in this direction at all," said the boys, with conviction in their manner.

"How do you know?" asked the officer.

"'Cause a gentleman told us so."

"Who? When? What gentleman?"

"A gentleman who met us a little while ago."

"How long ago? Who was he?"

"Don't know who he was," said Frank.

"When we were eating our snack," put in Willy, not to be left out.

"How was he dressed? Where was it? What sort of man was he?" eagerly inquired the leading trooper.

The boys proceeded to describe their friend, impressed by the intense interest accorded them by the listeners.

"He was a sort of a man with red hair, and wore a pair of gray breeches and an old pair of shoes, and was in his shirt-sleeves." Frank was the spokesman.

"And he had a gun—a long squirrel-gun," added Willy, "and he said he belonged to Colonel Marshall's regiment."

"Why, that 's Tim Mills. He 's a deserter himself," exclaimed the captain.

"No, he ain't—*he* ain't any deserter," protested both at once. "He is a mighty brave soldier, and he 's been home on a furlough to get well of a wound on his leg where he was shot."

"Yes, and it ain't well yet, but he 's going back to his command to-night or to-morrow morning; and he's got another wound in his side where a Yankee ran him through with his sword. We know *he* ain't any deserter."

"How do you know all this?" asked the officer.

"He told us so himself, just now—a little while ago, that is," said the boys.

The man laughed.

"Why, he 's fooled you to death. That 's Tim himself, that 's been doing all the devilment about here. He is the worst deserter in the whole gang."

"We saw the wound on his shoulder," declared the boys, still doubting.

"I know it; he 's got one there,—that 's what I know him by. Which way did he go,—and how long has it been?"

"He went that way, down in the woods; and it 's been some time. He 's got away now."

The lads by this time were almost convinced of their mistake; but they could not prevent their sympathy from being on the side of their late agreeable companion.

"We'll catch the rascal," declared the leader, very fiercely. "Come on, men,—he can't have gone far;" and he wheeled his horse about and dashed back up the road at a great pace, followed by his men. The boys were half inclined to follow and aid in the capture; but Frank, after a moment's thought, said solemnly:

"No, Willy; an Arab never betrays a man who has eaten his salt. This man has broken bread with us; we cannot give him up. I don't think we ought to have told about him as much as we did."

This was an argument not to be despised.

A little later, as the boys trudged home, they heard the horns blowing again a regular "toot-toot" for "Millindy." It struck them that supper followed dinner very quickly in Holetown.

When the troop passed by in the evening the men were in very bad humor. They had had a fruitless addition to their ride, and some of them were inclined to say that the boys had never seen any man at all, which the boys thought was pretty silly, as the man had eaten at least two-thirds of their lunch.

Somehow the story got out, and Hugh was very scornful because the boys had given their lunch to a deserter.

CHAPTER VIII.

AS time went by the condition of things at Oakland changed—as it did everywhere else. The boys' mother, like all the other ladies of the country, was so devoted to the cause that she gave to the soldiers until there was nothing left. After that there was a failure of the crops, and the immediate necessities of the family and the hands on the place were great.

There was no sugar nor coffee nor tea. These luxuries had been given up long before. An attempt was made to manufacture sugar out of the sorghum, or sugar-cane, which was now being cultivated as an experiment; but it proved unsuccessful, and molasses made from the cane was the only sweetening. The boys, however, never liked anything sweetened with molasses, so they gave up everything that had molasses in it. Sassafras tea was tried as a substitute for tea, and a drink made out of parched corn and wheat, of burnt sweet potato and other things, in the place of coffee; but none of them were fit to drink—at least so the boys thought. The wheat crop proved a failure; but the corn turned out very fine, and the boys learned to live on corn bread, as there was no wheat bread.

The soldiers still came by, and the house was often full of

young officers who came to see the boys' cousins. The boys used to ride the horses to and from the stables, and, being perfectly fearless, became very fine riders.

Several times, among the visitors, came the young colonel who had commanded the regiment that had camped at the bridge the first year of the war. It did not seem to the boys that Cousin Belle liked him, for she took much longer to dress when he came; and if there were other officers present she would take very little notice of the colonel.

Both boys were in love with her, and after considerable hesitation had written her a joint letter to tell her so, at which she laughed heartily and kissed them both and called them her sweethearts. But, though they were jealous of several young officers who came from time to time, they felt sorry for the colonel,—their cousin was so mean to him. They were on the best terms with him and had announced their intention of going into his regiment if only the war should last long enough. When he came there was always a scramble to get his horse; though of all who came to Oakland he rode the wildest horses, as both boys knew by practical experience.

At length the soldiers moved off too far to permit them to come on visits, and things were very dull. So it was for a long while.

But one evening in May, about sunset, as the boys were playing in the yard, a man came riding through the place on the way to Richmond. His horse showed that he had been riding hard. He asked the nearest way to "Ground-Squirrel Bridge." The Yankees, he said, were coming. It was a raid. He had ridden ahead of them, and had left them about Greenbay depot, which they had set on fire. He was in too great a hurry to stop and get something to eat, and he rode off, leaving much excitement behind him; for Greenbay was only eight miles away, and Oakland lay right between two roads to Richmond, down one or the other of which the party of raiders must certainly pass.

It was the first time the boys ever saw their mother exhibit so much emotion as she then did. She came to the door and called:

"Balla, come here." Her voice sounded to the boys a little strained and troubled, and they ran up the steps and stood by her. Balla came to the portico, and looked up with an air of inquiry. He, too, showed excitement.

"Balla, I want you to know that if you wish to go, you can do so."

"Hi, Mistis——" began Balla, with an air of reproach; but she cut him short and kept on.

"I want you all to know it." She was speaking now so as to be heard by the cook and the maids who were standing about the yard listening to her. "I want you all to know it —every one on the place! You can go if you wish; but, if you go, you can never come back!"

"Hi, Mistis," broke in Uncle Balla, "whar is I got to go? I wuz born on dis place an' I 'spec' to die here, an' be buried right *yonder;*" and he turned and pointed up to the dark clumps of trees that marked the graveyard on the hill, a half mile away, where the colored people were buried. "Dat I does," he affirmed positively. "Y' all sticks by us, and we 'll stick by you."

"I know I ain' gwine nowhar wid no Yankees or nothin'," said Lucy Ann, in an undertone.

"Dee tell me dee got hoofs and horns," laughed one of the women in the yard.

The boys' mother started to say something further to Balla, but though she opened her lips, she did not speak; she turned suddenly and walked into the house and into her chamber, where she shut the door behind her. The boys thought she was angry, but when they softly followed her a few minutes afterward, she got up hastily from where she had been kneeling beside the bed, and they saw that she had been crying. A murmur under the window called them back to the portico. It had begun to grow dark; but a bright spot was glowing on the horizon, and on this every one's gaze was fixed.

"Where is it, Balla? What is it?" asked the boys' mother, her voice no longer strained and harsh, but even softer than usual.

"It's the depot, madam. They 's burnin' it. That man told me they was burnin' ev'ywhar they went."

"Will they be here to-night?" asked his mistress.

"No, marm; I don' hardly think they will. That man

said they could n't travel more than thirty miles a day; but they 'ell be plenty of 'em here to-morrow—to breakfast." He gave a nervous sort of laugh.

"Here,—you all come here," said their mistress to the servants. She went to the smoke-house and unlocked it. "Go in there and get down the bacon—take a piece, each of you." A great deal was still left. "Balla, step here." She called him aside and spoke earnestly in an undertone.

"Yes 'm, that 's so; that 's jes' what I wuz gwine do," the boys heard him say.

Their mother sent the boys out. She went and locked herself in her room, but they heard her footsteps as she turned about within, and now and then they heard her opening and shutting drawers and moving chairs.

In a little while she came out.

"Frank, you and Willy go and tell Balla to come to the chamber door. He may be out in the stable."

They dashed out, proud to bear so important a message. They could not find him, but an hour later they heard him coming from the stable. He at once went into the house. They rushed into the chamber, where they found the door of the closet open.

"Balla, come in here," called their mother from within. "Have you got them safe?" she asked.

"Yes 'm; jes' as safe as they kin be. I want to be 'bout here when they come, or I 'd go down an' stay whar they is."

"What is it?" asked the boys.

"Where is the best place to put that?" she said, pointing to a large, strong box in which, they knew, the finest silver was kept; indeed, all excepting what was used every day on the table.

"Well, I declar', Mistis, that 's hard to tell," said the old driver, "without it 's in the stable."

"They may burn that down."

"That 's so; you might bury it under the floor of the smoke-house?"

"I have heard that they always look for silver there," said the boys' mother. "How would it do to bury it in the garden?"

"That 's the very place I was gwine name," said Balla, with flattering approval. "They can't burn *that* down, and if they gwine dig for it then they 'll have to dig a long time before they git over that big garden." He stooped and lifted up one end of the box to test its weight.

"I thought of the other end of the flower-bed, between the big rose-bush and the lilac."

"That 's the very place I had in my mind," declared the old man. "They won' never fine it dyah!"

"We know a good place," said the boys both together: "it 's a heap better than that. It 's where we bury our treasures when we play 'Black-beard the Pirate.'"

"Very well," said their mother; "I don't care to know where it is until after to-morrow, anyhow. I know I can trust you," she added, addressing Balla.

"Yes 'm, you know dat," said he, simply. "I 'll jes' go an' git my hoe."

"The garden hasn't got a roof to it, has it, Unc' Balla?" asked Willy, quietly.

"Go 'way from here, boy," said the old man, making a sweep at him with his hand. "That boy ain' never done talkin' 'bout that thing yit," he added, with a pleased laugh, to his mistress.

"And you ain't ever given me all those chickens either," responded Willy, forgetting his grammar.

"Oh, well, I 'm *gwi'* do it; ain't you hear me say I 'm gwine do it?" he laughed as he went out.

The boys were too excited to get sleepy before the silver was hidden. Their mother told them they might go down into the garden and help Balla, on condition that they would not talk.

"That 's the way we always do when we bury the treasure. Ain't it, Willy?" asked Frank.

"If a man speaks, it 's death!" declared Willy, slapping his hand on his side as if to draw a sword, striking a theatrical attitude and speaking in a deep voice.

"Give the 'galleon' to us," said Frank.

"No; be off with you," said their mother.

"That ain't the way," said Frank. "A pirate never digs the hole until he has his treasure at hand. To do so would prove him but a novice; would n't it, Willy?"

"Well, I leave it all to you, my little Buccaneers," said

their mother, laughing. "I'll take care of the spoons and forks we use every day. I 'll just hide them away in a hole somewhere."

The boys started off after Balla with a shout, but remembered their errand and suddenly hushed down to a little squeal of delight at being actually engaged in burying treasure—real silver. It seemed too good to be true, and withal there was a real excitement about it, for how could they know but that some one might watch them from some hiding-place, or might even fire into them as they worked?

They met the old fellow as he was coming from the carriage-house with a hoe and a spade in his hands. He was on his way to the garden in a very straightforward manner, but the boys made him understand that to bury treasure it was necessary to be particularly secret, and after some little grumbling, Balla humored them.

The difficulty of getting the box of silver out of the house secretly, whilst all the family were up, and the servants were moving about, was so great that this part of the affair had to be carried on in a manner different from the usual programme of pirates of the first water. Even the boys had to admit this; and they yielded to old Balla's advice on this point, but made up for it by additional formality, ceremony, and secrecy in pointing out the spot where the box was to be hid.

Old Balla was quite accustomed to their games and fun—their "pranks," as he called them. He accordingly yielded willingly when they marched him to a point at the lower end of the yard, on the opposite side from the garden, and left him. But he was inclined to give trouble when they both reappeared with a gun, and in a whisper announced that they must march first up the ditch which ran by the spring around the foot of the garden.

"Look here, boys; I ain' got time to fool with you chillern," said the old man. "Ain't you hear your ma tell me she 'pend on me to bury that silver what yo' gran'ma and gran'pa used to eat off o'—an' don' wan' nobody to know nothin' 'bout it? An' y' all comin' here with guns, like you huntin' squ'rr'ls, an' now talkin' 'bout wadin' in the ditch!"

"But, Unc' Balla, that's the way all buccaneers do," protested Frank.

"Yes, buccaneers always go by water," said Willy.

"And we can stoop in the ditch and come in at the far end of the garden, so nobody can see us," added Frank.

"Bookanear or bookafar,—I'se gwine in dat garden and dig a hole wid my hoe, an' I is too ole to be wadin' in a ditch like chillern. I got the misery in my knee now, so bad I'se sca'cely able to stand. I don't know huccome y' all ain't satisfied with the place you' ma an' I done pick, anyways."

This was too serious a mutiny for the boys. So it was finally agreed that one gun should be returned to the office, and that they should enter by the gate, after which Balla was to go with the boys by the way they should show him, and see the spot they thought of.

They took him down through the weeds around the garden, crouching under the rose-bushes, and at last stopped at a spot under the slope, completely surrounded by shrubbery.

"Here is the spot," said Frank in a whisper, pointing under one of the bushes.

"It's in a line with the longest limb of the big oak-tree by the gate," added Willy, "and when this locust bush and that cedar grow to be big trees, it will be just half-way between them."

As this seemed to Balla a very good place, he set to work at once to dig, the two boys helping him as well as they could. It took a great deal longer to dig the hole in the dark than they had expected, and when they got back to the house everything was quiet.

The boys had their hats pulled over their eyes, and had turned their jackets inside out to disguise themselves.

"It's a first-rate place! Ain't it, Unc' Balla?" they said, as they entered the chamber where their mother and aunt were waiting for them.

"Do you think it will do, Balla?" their mother asked.

"Oh, yes, madam; it's far enough, an' they got mighty comical ways to get dyah, wadin' in ditch an' things—it will do. I ain' sho' I kin fin' it ag'in myself." He was not particularly enthusiastic. Now, however, he shouldered the box, with a grunt at its weight, and the party went slowly out through the back door into the dark. The glow of the burning depot was still visible in the west.

Then it was decided that Willy should go before—he said

to "reconnoitre," Balla said "to open the gate and lead the way,"—and that Frank should bring up the rear.

They trudged slowly on through the darkness, Frank and Willy watching on every side, old Balla stooping under the weight of the big box.

After they were some distance in the garden they heard, or thought they heard, a sound back at the gate, but decided that it was nothing but the latch clicking; and they went on down to their hiding place.

In a little while the black box was well settled in the hole, and the dirt was thrown upon it. The replaced earth made something of a mound, which was unfortunate. They had not thought of this; but they covered it with leaves, and agreed that it was so well hidden, the Yankees would never dream of looking there.

"Unc' Balla, where are your horses?" asked one of the boys.

"'That's for me to know, an' them to find out what kin," replied the old fellow with a chuckle of satisfaction.

The whole party crept back out of the garden, and the boys were soon dreaming of buccaneers and pirates.

CHAPTER IX.

THE boys were not sure that they had even fallen asleep when they heard Lucy Ann call, outside. They turned over to take another nap. She was coming up to the door. No, for it was a man's step, it must be Uncle Balla's; they heard horses trampling and people talking. In a second the door was flung open, and a man strode into the room followed by one, two, a half-dozen others, all white and all in uniform. They were Yankees. The boys were too frightened to speak. They thought they were arrested for hiding the silver.

"Get up, you lazy little rebels," cried one of the intruders, not unpleasantly. As the boys were not very quick in obeying, being really too frightned to do more than sit up in bed, the man caught the mattress by the end, and lifting it with a jerk emptied them and all the bedclothes out into the middle of the floor in a heap. At this all the other men laughed. A minute more and he had drawn his sword. The boys expected no less than to be immediately killed. They were almost paralyzed. But instead of plunging his sword into them, the man began to stick it into the mattresses and to rip them up; while others pulled open the drawers of the bureau and pitched the things on the floor.

The boys felt themselves to be in a very exposed and defenceless condition; and Willy, who had become tangled in the bedclothes, and had been a little hurt in falling, now that the strain was somewhat over, began to cry.

In a minute a shadow darkened the doorway and their mother stood in the room.

"Leave the room instantly!" she cried. "Are n't you ashamed to frighten children!"

"We have n't hurt the brats," said the man with the sword, good-naturedly.

"Well, you terrify them to death. It 's just as bad. Give me those clothes!" and she sprang forward and snatched the boys' clothes from the hands of a man who had taken them up. She flung the suits to the boys, who lost no time in slipping into them.

They had at once recovered their courage in the presence of their mother. She seemed to them, as she braved the intruders, the grandest person they had ever seen. Her face was white, but her eyes were like coals of fire. They were very glad she had never looked or talked so to them.

When they got outdoors the yard was full of soldiers. They were upon the porches, in the entry, and in the house. The smoke-house was open and so were the doors of all the other outhouses, and now and then a man passed, carrying some article which the boys recognized.

In a little while the soldiers had taken everything they

could carry conveniently, and even things which must have caused them some inconvenience. They had secured all the bacon that had been left in the smoke-house, as well as all other eatables they could find. It was a queer sight, to see the fellows sitting on their horses with a ham or a pair of fowls tied to one side of the saddle and an engraving, or a package of books, or some ornament, to the other.

A new party of men had by this time come up from the direction of the stables.

"Old man, come here!" called some of them to Balla, who was standing near expostulating with the men who were about the fire.

"Who?—me?" asked Balla.

"B'ain't you the carriage driver?"

"Ain't I the keridge driver?"

Yes, *you;* we know you are, so you need not be lying about it."

"Hi! yes; I the keridge driver. Who say I ain't?"

"Well, where have you hid those horses? Come, we want to know, quick," said the fellow roughly, taking out his pistol in a threatening way.

The old man's eyes grew wide. "Hi! befo' de Lord! Marster, how I know anything of the horses ef they ain't in the stable,—there's where we keep horses!"

"Here, you come with us. We won't have no foolin' 'bout this," said his questioner, seizing him by the shoulder and jerking him angrily around. "If you don't show us

"GENTLEMEN, MARSTERS, DON'T TECK MY HORSES, EF YOU PLEASE," SAID UNCLE BALLA.

pretty quick where those horses are, we 'll put a bullet or two into you. March off there!"

He was backed by a half-a-dozen more, but the pistol, which was at old Balla's head, was his most efficient ally.

"Hi! Marster, don't pint dat thing at me that way. I ain't ready to die yit—an' I ain' like dem things, noways," protested Balla.

There is no telling how much further his courage could have withstood their threats, for the boys' mother made her appearance. She was about to bid Balla show where the horses were, when a party rode into the yard leading them.

"Hi! there are Bill and John, now," exclaimed the boys, recognizing the black carriage-horses which were being led along.

"Well, ef dee ain't got 'em, sho' 'nough!" exclaimed the old driver, forgetting his fear of the cocked pistols.

"Gentlemen, marsters, don't teck my horses, ef you *please*," he pleaded, pushing through the group that surrounded him, and approaching the man who led the horses.

They only laughed at him.

Both the boys ran to their mother, and, flinging their arms about her, burst out crying.

In a few minutes the men started off, riding across the fields; and in a little while not a soldier was in sight.

"I wish Marse William could see you ridin' 'cross them

fields," said Balla, looking after the retiring troop in futile indignation.

Investigation revealed the fact that every horse and mule on the plantation had been carried off, except only two or three old mules, which were evidently considered not worth taking.

CHAPTER X.

AFTER this, times were very hard on the plantation. But the boys' mother struggled to provide as best she could for the family and hands. She used to ride all over the county to secure the supplies which were necessary for their support; one of the boys usually being her escort and riding behind her on one of the old mules that the raiders had left. In this way the boys became acquainted with the roads of the county and even with all the bridle-paths in the neighborhood of their home. Many of these were dim enough too, running through stretches of pine forest, across old fields which were little better than jungle, along gullies, up ditches, and through woods mile after mile. They were generally useful only to a race, such as the negroes, which had an instinct for direction like that shown by some animals; but the boys learned to follow them unerringly, and soon became as skilful in "keepin' de parf" as any night-walker on the plantation.

As the year passed the times grew harder and harder, and the expeditions made by the boys' mother became longer and longer, and more and more frequent.

The meat gave out, and, worst of all, they had no hogs left for next year. The plantation usually subsisted on bacon;

but now there was not a pig left on the place—unless the old wild sow in the big woods (who had refused to be "driven up" the fall before) still survived, which was doubtful; for the most diligent search was made for her without success, and it was conceded that even she had fallen prey to the deserters. Nothing was heard of her for months.

One day, in the autumn, the boys were out hunting in the big woods, in the most distant and wildest part, where they sloped down toward a little marshy branch that ran into the river a mile or two away.

It was a very dry spell and squirrels were hard to find, owing, the boys agreed, to the noise made in tramping through the dry leaves. Finally, they decided to station themselves each at the foot of a hickory and wait for the squirrels. They found two large hickory trees not too far apart, and took their positions each on the ground, with his back to a tree.

It was very dull, waiting, and a half-whispered colloquy was passing between them as to the advisability of giving it up, when a faint "cranch, cranch, cranch," sounded in the dry leaves. At first the boys thought it was a squirrel, and both of them grasped their guns. Then the sound came again, but this time there appeared to be, not one, but a number of animals, rustling slowly along.

"What is it?" asked Frank of Willy, whose tree was a little nearer the direction from which the sound came.

"'Tain't anything but some cows or sheep, I believe,"

said Willy, in a disappointed tone. The look of interest died out of Frank's face, but he still kept his eyes in the direction of the sound, which was now very distinct. The underbrush, however, was too thick for them to see anything. At length Willy rose and pushed his way rapidly through the bushes toward the animals. There was a sudden "oof, oof," and Frank heard them rushing back down through the woods toward the marsh.

"Somebody's hogs," he muttered, in disgust.

"Frank! Frank!" called Willy, in a most excited tone.

"What?"

"It 's the old spotted sow, and she 's got a lot of pigs with her—great big shoats, nearly grown!"

Frank sprang up and ran through the bushes.

"At least six of 'em!"

"Let 's follow 'em!"

"All right."

The boys, stooping their heads, struck out through the bushes in the direction from which the yet retreating animals could still be heard.

"Let 's shoot 'em."

"All right."

On they kept as hard as they could. What great news it was! What royal game!

"It 's like hunting wild boars, is n't it?" shouted Willy, joyfully.

They followed the track left by the animals in the leaves

kicked up in their mad flight. It led down over the hill through the thicket, and came to an end at the marsh which marked the beginning of the swamp. Beyond that it could not be traced ; but it was evident that the wild hogs had taken refuge in the impenetrable recesses of the marsh which was their home.

CHAPTER XI.

AFTER circling the edge of the swamp for some time the boys, as it was now growing late, turned toward home. They were full of their valuable discovery, and laid all sorts of plans for the capture of the hogs. They would not tell even their mother, as they wished to surprise her. They were, of course, familiar with all the modes of trapping game, as described in the story books, and they discussed them all. The easiest way to get the hogs was to shoot them, and this would be the most "fun;" but it would never do, for the meat would spoil. When they reached home they hunted up Uncle Balla and told him about their discovery. He was very much inclined to laugh at them. The hogs they had seen were nothing, he told them, but some of the neighbors' hogs which had wandered into the woods.

When the boys went to bed they talked it over once more, and determined that next day they would thoroughly explore the woods and the swamp also, as far as they could.

The following afternoon, therefore, they set out, and made immediately for that part of the woods where they had seen and heard the hogs the day before. One of them carried a gun and the other a long jumping-pole. After finding the trail they followed it straight down to the swamp.

Rolling their trousers up above their knees, they waded boldly in, selecting an opening between the bushes which looked like a hog-path. They proceeded slowly, for the briers were so thick in many places that they could hardly make any progress at all when they neared the branch. So they turned and worked their way painfully down the stream. At last, however, they reached a place where the brambles and bushes seemed to form a perfect wall before them. It was impossible to get through.

"Let 's go home," said Willy. "'Tain't any use to try to get through there. My legs are scratched all to pieces now."

"Let 's try and get out here," said Frank, and he turned from the wall of brambles. They crept along, springing from hummock to hummock. Presently they came to a spot where the oozy mud extended at least eight or ten feet before the next tuft of grass.

"How am I to get the gun across?" asked Willy, dolefully.

"That 's a fact! It 's too far to throw it, even with the caps off."

At length they concluded to go back for a piece of log they had seen, and to throw this down so as to lessen the distance.

They pulled the log out of the sand, carried it to the muddy spot, and threw it into the mud where they wanted it.

Frank stuck his pole down and felt until he had what he

thought a secure hold on it, fixed his eye on the tuft of grass beyond, and sprang into air.

As he jumped the pole slipped from its insecure support into the miry mud, and Frank, instead of landing on the hummock for which he had aimed, lost his direction, and soused flat on his side with a loud "spa-lash," in the water and mud three feet to the left.

He was a queer object as he staggered to his feet in the quagmire; but at the instant a loud "oof, oof," came from the thicket, not a dozen yards away, and the whole herd of hogs, roused, by his fall, from slumber in their muddy lair, dashed away through the swamp with "oofs" of fear.

"There they go, there they go!" shouted both boys, eagerly,—Willy, in his excitement, splashing across the perilous-looking quagmire, and finding it not so deep as it had looked.

"There 's where they go in and out," exclaimed Frank, pointing to a low round opening, not more than eighteen inches high, a little further beyond them, which formed an arch in the almost solid wall of brambles surrounding the place.

As it was now late they returned home, resolving to wait until the next afternoon before taking any further steps. There was not a pound of bacon to be obtained anywhere in the country for love or money, and the flock of sheep was almost gone.

Their mother's anxiety as to means for keeping her dependents from starving was so great that the boys were on the point of telling her what they knew; and when they heard her wishing she had a few hogs to fatten, they could scarcely keep from letting her know their plans. At last they had to jump up, and run out of the room.

Next day the boys each hunted up a pair of old boots which they had used the winter before. The leather was so dry and worn that the boots hurt their growing feet cruelly, but they brought the boots along to put on when they reached the swamp. This time, each took a gun, and they also carried an axe, for now they had determined on a plan for capturing the hogs.

"I wish we had let Peter and Cole come," said Willy, dolefully, sitting on the butt end of a log they had cut, and wiping his face on his sleeve.

"Or had asked Uncle Balla to help us," added Frank.

"They 'd be certain to tell all about it."

"Yes; so they would."

They settled down in silence, and panted.

"I tell you what we ought to do! Bait the hog-path, as you would for fish." This was the suggestion of the angler, Frank.

"With what?"

"Acorns."

The acorns were tolerably plentiful around the roots of the big oaks, so the boys set to work to pick them up. It was an easier job than cutting the log, and it was not long before each had his hat full.

As they started down to the swamp, Frank exclaimed, suddenly, "Look there, Willy!"

Willy looked, and not fifty yards away, with their ends resting on old stumps, were three or four "hacks," or piles of rails, which had been mauled the season before and left there, probably having been forgotten or overlooked.

Willy gave a hurrah, while bending under the weight of a large rail.

At the spot where the hog-path came out of the thicket they commenced to build their trap.

First they laid a floor of rails; then they built a pen, five or six rails high, which they strengthened with "outriders." When the pen was finished, they pried up the side nearest the thicket, from the bottom rail, about a foot; that is, high enough for the animals to enter. This they did by means of two rails, using one as a fulcrum and one as a lever, having shortened them enough to enable the work to be done from inside the pen.

The lever they pulled down at the farther end until it touched the bottom of the trap, and fastened it by another rail, a thin one, run at right-angles to the lever, and across the pen. This would slip easily when pushed away from the gap, and needed to be moved only about an inch to slip from the end of the lever and release it; the weight of the pen would then close the gap. Behind this rail the acorns were to be thrown ; and the hogs, in trying to get the bait, woulc push the rail, free the lever or trigger, and the gap would b closed by the fall of the pen when the lever was released.

It was nearly night when the boys finished.

They scattered a portion of the acorns for bait along th path and up into the pen, to toll the hogs in. The rest the strewed inside the pen, beyond their sliding rail.

They could scarcely tear themselves away from the pen but it was so late they had to hurry home.

Next day was Sunday. But Monday morning, by day light, they were up and went out with their guns, apparentl to hunt squirrels. They went, however, straight to their trap As they approached they thought they heard the hogs grunt ing in the pen. Willy was sure of it ; and they ran as harc as they could. But there were no hogs there. After goin every morning and evening for two weeks, there never hac been even an acorn missed, so they stopped their visits.

Peter and Cole found out about the pen, and then th servants learned of it, and the boys were joked and laughe at unmercifully.

" I believe them boys is distracted," said old Balla, in th kitchen ; " settin' a pen in them woods for to ketch hogs,— with the gap open ! Think hogs goin' stay in pen with ga open—ef any wuz dyah to went in ! "

" Well, you come out and help us hunt for them," sai the boys to the old driver.

" Go 'way, boy, I ain' got time foolin' wid you chillern

buildin' pen in swamp. There ain't no hogs in them woods, onless they got in dyah sence las' fall."

"You saw 'em, did n't you, Willy?" declared Frank.

"Yes, I did."

"Go 'way. Don't you know, ef that old sow had been in them woods the boys would have got her up las' fall—an' ef they had n't, she 'd come up long befo' this?"

"Mister Hall ketch you boys puttin' his hogs up in pen, he 'll teck you up," said Lucy Ann, in her usual teasing way.

This was too much for the boys to stand after all they had done. Uncle Balla must be right. They would have to admit it. The hogs must have belonged to some one else. And their mother was in such desperate straits about meat!

Lucy Ann's last shot, about catching Mr. Hall's hogs, took effect; and the boys agreed that they would go out some afternoon and pull the pen down.

The next afternoon they took their guns, and started out on a squirrel-hunt.

They did not have much luck, however.

"Let 's go by there, and pull the old pen down," said Frank, as they started homeward from the far side of the woods.

"It 's out of the way,—let the old thing rip."

"We 'd better pull it down. If a hog were to be caught there, it would n't do."

"I wish he would!—but there ain't any hogs going to get caught," growled Willy.

"He might starve to death."

This suggestion persuaded Willy, who could not bear to have anything suffer.

So they sauntered down toward the swamp.

As they approached it, a squirrel ran up a tree, and both boys were after it in a second. They were standing, one on each side of the tree, gazing up, trying to get a sight of the little animal among the gray branches, when a sound came to the ears of both of them at the same moment.

"What 's that?" both asked together.

"It 's hogs, grunting."

"No, they are fighting. They are in the swamp. Let 's run," said Willy.

"No; we 'll scare them away. They may be near the trap," was Frank's prudent suggestion. "Let 's creep up."

"I hear young pigs squealing. Do you think they are ours?"

The squirrel was left, flattened out and trembling on top of a large limb, and the boys stole down the hill toward the pen. The hogs were not in sight, though they could be heard grunting and scuffling. They crept closer. Willy crawled through a thick clump of bushes, and sprang to his feet with a shout. "We 've got 'em! We 've got 'em!" he cried, running toward the pen, followed by Frank.

Sure enough! There they were, fast in the pen, fighting and snorting to get out, and tearing around with the bristles high on their round backs, the old sow and seven large young hogs; while a litter of eight little pigs, as the boys ran up, squeezed through the rails, and, squealing, dashed away into the grass.

The hogs were almost frantic at the sight of the boys, and rushed madly at the sides of the pen; but the boys had made it too strong to be broken.

After gazing at their capture awhile, and piling a few more outriders on the corners of the pen to make it more secure, the two trappers rushed home. They dashed breathless and panting into their mother's room, shouting, "We 've got 'em!—we 've got 'em!" and, seizing her, began to dance up and down with her.

In a little while the whole plantation was aware of the capture, and old Balla was sent out with them to look at the hogs to make sure they did not belong to some one else,—as he insisted they did. The boys went with him. It was quite dark when he returned, but as he came in the proof of the boys' success was written on his face. He was in a broad grin. To his mistress's inquiry he replied, "Yes, 'm, they 's got 'em, sho' 'nough. They 's the beatenes' boys!"

For some time afterward he would every now and then break into a chuckle of amused content and exclaim, "Them 's right smart chillern." And at Christmas, when the hogs were killed, this was the opinion of the whole plantation.

CHAPTER XII.

THE gibes of Lucy Ann, and the occasional little thrusts of Hugh about the "deserter business," continued and kept the boys stirred up. At length they could stand it no longer. It was decided between them that they must retrieve their reputations by capturing a real deserter and turning him over to the conscript-officer whose office was at the depot.

Accordingly, one Saturday they started out on an expedition, the object of which was to capture a deserter though they should die in the attempt.

The conscript-guard had been unusually active lately, and it was said that several deserters had been caught.

The boys turned in at their old road, and made their way into Holetown. Their guns were loaded with large slugs, and they felt the ardor of battle thrill them as they marched along down the narrow roadway. They were trudging on when they were hailed by name from behind. Turning, they saw their friend Tim Mills, coming along at the same slouching gait in which he always walked. His old single-barrel gun was thrown across his arm, and he looked a little rustier than on the day he had shared their lunch. The boys held a little whispered conversation, and decided on a treaty of friendship.

"Good-mornin'," he said, on coming up to them. "How's your ma?"

"Good-morning. She's right well."

"What y' all doin'? Huntin' d'serters agin?" he asked.

"Yes. Come on and help us catch them."

"No; I can't do that—exactly;—but I tell you what I *can* do. I can tell you whar one is!"

The boys' faces glowed. "All right!"

"Let me see," he began, reflectively, chewing a stick. "Does y' all know Billy Johnson?"

The boys did not know him.

"You *sure* you don't know him? He's a tall, long fellow, 'bout forty years old, and breshes his hair mighty slick; got a big nose, and a gap-tooth, and a mustache. He lives down in the lower neighborhood."

Even after this description the boys failed to recognize him.

"Well, he's the feller. I can tell you right whar he is, this minute. He did me a mean trick, an' I'm gwine to give him up. Come along."

"What did he do to you?" inquired the boys, as they followed him down the road.

"Why—he—; but 't 's no use to be rakin' it up agin. You know he always passes hisself off as one o' the conscrip'-guards,—that 's his dodge. Like as not, that's what he 's gwine try and put off on y' all now; but don't you let him fool you."

"We're not going to," said the boys.

"He rigs hisself up in a uniform—jes' like as not he stole it, too,—an' goes roun' foolin' people, meckin' out he's such a soldier. If he fools with me, I'm gwine to finish him!" Here Tim gripped his gun fiercely.

The boys promised not to be fooled by the wily Johnson. All they asked was to have him pointed out to them.

"Don't you let him put up any game on you 'bout bein' a conscrip'-guard hisself," continued their friend.

"No, indeed we won't. We are obliged to you for telling us."

"He ain't so very fur from here. He's mighty tecken up with John Hall's gal, and is tryin' to meck out like he's Gen'l Lee hisself, an' she ain't got no mo' sense than to b'lieve him."

"Why, we heard, Mr. Mills, she was going to marry *you*."

"Oh, no, *I* ain't a good enough soldier for her; she wants to marry *Gen'l Lee*."

The boys laughed at his dry tone.

As they walked along they consulted how the capture should be made.

"I tell you how to take him," said their companion. "He is a monstrous coward, and all you got to do is jest to bring your guns down on him. I would n't shoot him—'nless he tried to run; but if he did that, when he got a little distance I'd pepper him about his legs. Make him give up his sword and pistol and don't let him ride; 'cause if you do, he'll git away. Make him walk—the rascal!"

The boys promised to carry out these kindly suggestions.

They soon came in sight of the little house where Mills said the deserter was. A soldier's horse was standing tied at the gate, with a sword hung from the saddle. The owner, in full uniform, was sitting on the porch.

"I can't go any furder," whispered their friend; "but that's him—that's 'Gen'l Lee'—the triflin' scoundrel!—loafin' 'roun' here 'sted o' goin' in the army! I b'lieve y' all is 'fraid to take him," eying the boys suspiciously.

"No, we ain't; you'll see," said both boys, fired at the doubt.

"All right; I'm goin' to wait right here and watch you. Go ahead."

The boys looked at the guns to see if they were all right, and marched up the road keeping their eyes on the enemy. It was agreed that Frank was to do the talking and give the orders.

They said not a word until they reached the gate. They could see a young woman moving about in the house, setting a table. At the gate they stopped, so as to prevent the man from getting to his horse.

The soldier eyed them curiously. "I wonder whose boys they is?" he said to himself. "They's certainly actin' comical! Playin' soldiers, I reckon."

"Cock your gun—easy," said Frank, in a low tone, suiting his own action to the word.

Willy obeyed.

"Come out here, if you please," Frank called to the man. He could not keep his voice from shaking a little, but the man rose and lounged out toward them. His prompt compliance reassured them.

They stood, gripping their guns and watching him as he advanced.

"Come outside the gate!" He did as Frank said.

"What do you want?" he asked impatiently.

"You are our prisoner," said Frank, sternly, dropping down his gun with the muzzle toward the captive, and giving a glance at Willy to see that he was supported.

"Your *what?* What do you mean?"

"We arrest you as a deserter."

How proud Willy was of Frank!

"Go 'way from here; I ain't no deserter. I'm a-huntin' for deserters, myself," the man replied, laughing.

Frank smiled at Willy with a nod, as much as to say, "You see,—just what Tim told us!"

"Ain't your name Mr. Billy Johnson?"

"Yes; that's my name."

"You are the man we're looking for. March down that road. But don't run,—if you do, we'll shoot you!"

As the boys seemed perfectly serious and the muzzles of both guns were pointing directly at him, the man began to think that they were in earnest. But he could hardly credit his senses. A suspicion flashed into his mind.

"Look here, boys," he said, rather angrily, "I don't want any of your foolin' with me. I'm too old to play with children. If you all don't go 'long home and stop giving me impudence, I'll slap you over!" He started angrily toward Frank. As he did so, Frank brought the gun to his shoulder.

"Stand back!" he said, looking along the barrel, right into the man's eyes. "If you move a step, I'll blow your head off!"

The soldier's jaw fell. He stopped and threw up his arm before his eyes.

"Hold on!" he called, "don't shoot! Boys, ain't you got better sense 'nt hat?"

"March on down that road. Willy, you get the horse," said Frank, decidedly.

The soldier glanced over toward the house. The voice of the young woman was heard singing a war song in a high key.

"Ef Millindy sees me, I'm a goner," he reflected. "Jes come down the road a little piece, will you?" he asked, persuasively.

"No talking,—march!" ordered Frank.

He looked at each of the boys; the guns still kept their perilous direction. The boys' eyes looked fiery to his surprised senses.

"Who is y' all?" he asked.

"We are two little Confederates! That's who we are," said Willy.

"Is any of your parents ever—ever been in a asylum?" he asked, as calmly as he could.

"That's none of your business," said Captain Frank "March on!"

The man cast a despairing glance toward the house, where "The years" were "creeping slowly by, Lorena," in a very high pitch,—and then moved on.

"I hope she ain't seen nothin'," he thought. "If I jest can git them guns away from 'em——"

Frank followed close behind him with his old gun held ready for need, and Willy untied the horse and led it. The bushes concealed them from the dwelling.

As soon as they were well out of sight of the house, Frank gave the order:

"Halt!" They all halted.

"Willy, tie the horse." It was done.

"I wonder if those boys is thinkin' 'bout shootin' me?" thought the soldier, turning and putting his hand on his pistol.

As he did so, Frank's gun came to his shoulder.

"Throw up your hands or you are a dead man." The hands went up.

"Willy, keep your gun on him, while I search him for any weapons." Willy cocked the old musket and brought it to bear on the prisoner.

"Little boy, don't handle that thing so reckless," the man expostulated. "Ef that musket was to go off, it might kill me!"

"No talking," demanded Frank, going up to him. "Hold up your hands. Willy, shoot him if he moves."

Frank drew a long pistol from its holster with an air of business. He searched carefully, but there was no more.

The fellow gritted his teeth. "If she ever hears of *this*, Tim's got her certain," he groaned; "but she won't never hear."

At a turn in the road his heart sank within him; for just around the curve they came upon Tim Mills sitting quietly on a stump. He looked at them with a quizzical eye, but said not a word.

The prisoner's face was a study when he recognized his rival and enemy. As Mills did not move, his courage returned.

"Good mornin', Tim," he said, with great politeness.

The man on the stump said nothing; he only looked on with complacent enjoyment.

"Tim, is these two boys crazy?" he asked slowly.

"They 're crazy 'bout shootin' deserters," replied Tim.

"Tim, tell 'em I ain't no deserter." His voice was full of entreaty.

"Well, if you ain't a d'serter, what you doin' outn the army?"

"You know——" began the fellow fiercely; but Tim

shifted his long single-barrel lazily into his hand and looked the man straight in the eyes, and the prisoner stopped.

"Yes, I know," said Tim with a sudden spark in his eyes. "An' *you* know," he added after a pause, during which his face resumed its usual listless look. "An' my edvice to you is to go 'long with them boys, if you don't want to git three loads of slugs in you. They *may* put 'em in you anyway. They's sort of 'stracted 'bout d'serters, and I can swear to it." He touched his forehead expressively.

"March on!" said Frank.

The prisoner, grinding his teeth, moved forward, followed by his guards.

As the enemies parted each man sent the same ugly look after the other.

"It's all over! He's got her," groaned Johnson. As they passed out of sight, Mills rose and sauntered somewhat briskly (for him) in the direction of John Hall's.

They soon reached a little stream, not far from the depot where the provost-guard was stationed. On its banks the man made his last stand; but his obstinacy brought a black muzzle close to his head with a stern little face behind it, and he was fain to march straight through the water, as he was ordered.

Just as he was emerging on the other bank, with his boots full of water and his trousers dripping, closely followed by Frank brandishing his pistol, a small body of soldiers rode up. They were the conscript-guard. Johnson's look was despairing.

FRANK AND WILLY CAPTURE A MEMBER OF THE CONSCRIPT-GUARD.

"Why, Billy, what in thunder——? Thought you were sick in bed!"

Another minute and the soldiers took in the situation by instinct—and Johnson's rage was drowned in the universal explosion of laughter.

The boys had captured a member of the conscript-guard.

In the midst of all, Frank and Willy, overwhelmed by their ridiculous error, took to their heels as hard as they could, and the last sounds that reached them were the roars of the soldiers as the scampering boys disappeared in a cloud of dust.

Johnson went back, in a few days, to see John Hall's daughter; but the young lady declared she would n't marry any man who let two boys make him wade through a creek; and a month or two later she married Tim Mills.

To all the gibes he heard on the subject of his capture, and they were many, Johnson made but one reply:

"Them boys 's had parents in a a—sylum, *sure!*"

CHAPTER XIII.

IT was now nearing the end of the third year of the war. Hugh was seventeen, and was eager to go into the army. His mother would have liked to keep him at home ; but she felt that it was her duty not to withhold anything, and Colonel Marshall offered Hugh a place with him. So a horse was bought, and Hugh went to Richmond and came back with a uniform and a sabre. The boys truly thought that General Lee himself was not so imposing or so great a soldier as Hugh. They followed him about like two pet dogs, and when he sat down they stood and gazed at him adoringly.

When Hugh rode away to the army it was harder to part with him than they had expected ; and though he had left them his gun and dog, to console them during his absence, it was difficult to keep from crying. Everyone on the plantation was moved. Uncle Balla, who up to the last moment had been very lively attending to the horse, as the young soldier galloped away sank down on the end of the steps of the office, and, dropping his hands on his knees, followed Hugh with his eyes until he disappeared over the hill. The old driver said nothing, but his face expressed a great deal.

The boys' mother cried a great deal, but it was generally when she was by herself.

"She 's afraid Hugh 'll be kilt," Willy said to Uncle Balla, in explanation of her tears,—the old servant having remarked that he "b'lieved she cried more when Hugh went away, than she did when Marse John and Marse William both went."

"Hi! war n't she 'fred they 'll be kilt, too?" he asked in some scorn.

This was beyond Willy's logic, so he pondered over it.

"Yes, but she 's afraid Hugh 'll be kilt, as *well* as them," he said finally, as the best solution of the problem.

It did not seem to wholly satisfy Uncle Balla's mind, for when he moved off he said, as though talking to himself:

"She sutn'ey is 'sot' on that boy. He 'll be a gen'l his-self, the first thing she know."

There was a bond of sympathy between Uncle Balla and his mistress which did not exist so strongly between her and any of the other servants. It was due perhaps to the fact that he was the companion and friend of her boys.

That winter the place where the army went into winter-quarters was some distance from Oakland; but the young officers used to ride over, from time to time, two or three together, and stay for a day or two.

Times were harder than they had been before, but the young people were as gay as ever.

The colonel, who had been dreadfully wounded in the summer, had been made a brigadier-general for gallantry. Hugh had received a slight wound in the same action. The

General had written to the boy's mother about him; but he had not been home. The General had gone back to his command. He had never been to Oakland since he was wounded.

One evening, the boys had just teased their Cousin Belle into reading them their nightly portion of "The Talisman," as they sat before a bright lightwood fire, when two horsemen galloped up to the gate, their horses splashed with mud from fetlocks to ears. In a second, Lucy Ann dashed headlong into the room, with her teeth gleaming:

"Here Marse Hugh, out here!"

There was a scamper to the door—the boys first, shouting at the tops of their voices, Cousin Belle next, and Lucy Ann close at her heels.

"Who 's with him, Lucy Ann?" asked Miss Belle, as they reached the passage-way, and heard several voices outside.

"The Cunnel's with 'im."

The young lady turned and fled up the steps as fast as she could.

"You see I brought my welcome with me," said the General, addressing the boy's mother, and laying his hand on his young aide's shoulder, as they stood, a little later, "thawing out" by the roaring log-fire in the sitting-room.

"You always bring that; but you are doubly welcome for bringing this young soldier back to me," said she, putting her arm affectionately around her son.

Just then the boys came rushing in from taking the horses

to the stable. They made a dive toward the fire to warm their little chapped hands.

"I told you Hugh war n't as tall as the General," said Frank, across the hearth to Willy.

"Who said he was?"

"You!"

"I did n't."

"You did."

They were a contradictory pair of youngsters, and their voices, pitched in a youthful treble, were apt in discussion to strike a somewhat higher key; but it did not follow that they were in an ill-humor merely because they contradicted each other.

"What *did* you say, if you did n't say that?" insisted Frank.

"I said he *looked* as if he *thought* himself as tall as the General," declared Willy, defiantly, oblivious in his excitement of the eldest brother's presence. There was a general laugh at Hugh's confusion; but Hugh had carried an order across a field under a hot fire, and had brought a regiment up in the nick of time, riding by its colonel's side in a charge which had changed the issue of the fight, and had a sabre wound in the arm to show for it. He could therefore afford to pass over such an accusation with a little tweak of Willy's ear.

"Where 's Cousin Belle?" asked Frank.

"I s'peck she 's putting on her fine clothes for the General to see. Did n't she run when she heard he was here!"

"Willy!" said his mother, reprovingly.

"Well, she did, Ma."

His mother shook her head at him; but the General put his hand on the boy, and drew him closer.

"You say she ran?" he asked, with a pleasant light in his eyes.

"Yes, sirree; she did *that*."

Just then the door opened, and their Cousin Belle entered the room. She looked perfectly beautiful. The greetings were very cordial—to Hugh especially. She threw her arms around his neck, and kissed him.

"You young hero!" she cried. "Oh, Hugh, I am so proud of you!"—kissing him again, and laughing at him, with her face glowing, and her big brown eyes full of light. "Where were you wounded? Oh! I was so frightened when I heard about it!"

"Where was it? Show it to us, Hugh; please do," exclaimed both boys at once, jumping around him, and pulling at his arm.

"Oh, Hugh, is it still very painful?" asked his cousin, her pretty face filled with sudden sympathy.

"Oh! no, it was nothing—nothing but a scratch," said Hugh, shaking the boys off, his expression being divided between feigned indifference and sheepishness, at this praise in the presence of his chief.

"No such thing, Miss Belle," put in the General, glad of the chance to secure her commendation. "It might have been very serious, and it was a splendid ride he made."

"Were you not ashamed of yourself to send him into such danger?" she said, turning on him suddenly. "Why did you not go yourself?"

The young man laughed. Her beauty entranced him. He had scars enough to justify him in keeping silence under her pretended reproach.

"Well, you see, I could n't leave the place where I was. I had to send some one, and I knew Hugh would do it. He led the regiment after the colonel and major fell—and he did it splendidly, too."

There was a chorus from the young lady and the boys together.

"Oh, Hugh, you hear what he says!" exclaimed the former, turning to her cousin. "Oh, I am so glad that he thinks so!" Then, recollecting that she was paying him the highest compliment, she suddenly began to blush, and turned once more to him. "Well, you talk as if you were surprised. Did you expect anything else?"

There was a fine scorn in her voice, if it had been real.

"Certainly not; you are all too clever at making an attack," he said coolly, looking her in the eyes. "But I have heard even of *your* running away," he added, with a twinkle in his eyes.

"When?" she asked quickly, with a little guilty color deepening in her face as she glanced at the boys. "I never did."

"Oh, she did!" exclaimed both boys in a breath, breaking in, now that the conversation was within their range. You ought to have seen her. She just *flew!*" exclaimed Frank.

The girl made a rush at the offender to stop him.

"He does n't know what he is talking about," she said, roguishly, over her shoulder.

"Yes, he does," called the other. "She was standing at the foot of the steps when you all came, and—oo—oo—oo—" the rest was lost as his cousin placed her hand close over his mouth.

"Here! here! run away! You are too dangerous. They don't know what they are talking about," she said, throwing a glance toward the young officer, who was keenly enjoying her confusion. Her hand slipped from Willie's mouth and he went on. "And when she heard it was you, she just clapped her hands and ran — oo — oo — umm."

"Here, Hugh, put them out," she said to that young man, who, glad to do her bidding, seized both miscreants by their arms and carried them out, closing the door after them.

Hugh bore the boys into the dining-room, where he kept them until supper-time.

After supper, the rest of the family dispersed, and the boys' mother invited them to come with her and Hugh to her own room, though they were eager to go and see the General, and were much troubled lest he should think their mother was rude in leaving him.

CHAPTER XIV.

THE next day was Sunday. The General and Hugh had but one day to stay. They were to leave at daybreak the following morning. They thoroughly enjoyed their holiday; at least the boys knew that Hugh did. They had never known him so affable with them. They did not see much of the General, after breakfast. He seemed to like to stay "stuck up in the house" all the time, talking to Cousin Belle; the boys thought this due to his lameness. Something had occurred, the boys did n't understand just what; but the General was on an entirely new footing with all of them, and their Cousin Belle was in some way concerned in the change. She did not any longer run from the General, and it seemed to them as though everyone acted as if he belonged to her. The boys did not altogether like the state of affairs. That afternoon, however, he and their Cousin Belle let the boys go out walking with them, and he was just as hearty as he could be; he made them tell him all about capturing the deserter, and about catching the hogs, and everything they did. They told him all about their "Robbers' Cave," down in the woods near where an old house had stood. It was between two ravines near a spring they had found. They had fixed up the "cave" with boards and old pieces of carpet "and everything," and they told him, as a secret, how to get to it through the pines without leaving a trail. He had to give the holy pledge of the "Brotherhood" before this could be divulged to him; but he took it with a solemnity which made the boys almost forgive the presence of their Cousin Belle. It was a little awkward at first that she was present; but as the "Constitution" provided only as to admitting men to the mystic knowledge, saying nothing about women, this difficulty was, on the General's suggestion, passed over, and the boys fully explained the location of the spot, and how to get there by turning off abruptly from the path through the big woods right at the pine thicket,—and all the rest of the way.

"'T ain't a 'sure-enough' cave," explained Willy; "but it 's 'most as good as one. The old rock fire-place is just like a cave."

"The gullies are so deep you can't get there except that one way," declared Frank.

"Even the Yankees could n't find you there," asserted Willy.

"I don't believe anybody could, after that; but I trust they will never have to try," laughed their Cousin Belle, with an anxious look in her bright eyes at the mere thought.

That night they were at supper, about eight o'clock, when something out-of-doors attracted the attention of the party around the table. It was a noise,—a something indefinable, but the talk and mirth stopped suddenly, and everybody listened.

There was a call, and the hurried steps of some one running, just outside the door, and Lucy Ann burst into the room, her face ashy pale.

"The yard's full o' mens—Yankees," she gasped, just as the General and Hugh rose from the table.

"How many are there?" asked both gentlemen.

"They 's all 'roun' the house ev'y which a-way."

The General looked at his sweetheart. She came to his side with a cry.

"Go up stairs to the top of the house," called the boys' mother.

"We can hide you; come with us," said the boys.

"Go up the back way, Frank 'n' Willy, to you-all's den," whispered Lucy Ann.

"That 's where we are going," said the boys as she went out.

"You all come on!" This to the General and Hugh.

"The rest of you take your seats," said the boys' mother.

All this had occupied only a few seconds. The soldiers followed the boys out by a side-door and dashed up the narrow stairs to the second-story just as a thundering knocking came at the front door. It was as dark as pitch, for candles were too scarce to burn more than one at a time.

"You run back," said Hugh to the boys, as they groped along. "There are too many of us. I know the way."

But it was too late; the noise down stairs told that the enemy was already in the house!

As the soldiers left the supper-room, the boys' mother had hastily removed two plates from the places and set two chairs back against the wall; she made the rest fill up the spaces, so that there was nothing to show that the two men had been there.

She had hardly taken her seat again, when the sound of heavy footsteps at the door announced the approach of the enemy. She herself rose and went to the door; but it was thrown open before she reached it and an officer in full Federal uniform strode in, followed by several men.

The commander was a tall young fellow, not older than the General. The lady started back somewhat startled, and there was a confused chorus of exclamations of alarm from the rest of those at the table. The officer, finding himself in the presence of ladies, removed his cap with a polite bow.

"I hope, madam, that you ladies will not be alarmed," he said. "You need be under no apprehension, I assure you." Even while speaking, his eye had taken a hasty survey of the room.

"We desire to see General Marshall, who is at present in this house, and I am sorry to have to include your son in my requisition. We know that they are here, and if they are given us, I promise you that nothing shall be disturbed."

"You appear to be so well instructed that I can add little to your information," said the mistress of the house, haughtily. "I am glad to say, however, that I hardly think you will find them."

" Madam, I know they are here," said the young soldier positively, but with great politeness. " I have positive information to that effect. They arrived last evening and have not left since. Their horses are still in the stable. I am sorry to be forced to do violence to my feelings, but I must search the house. Come, men."

" I doubt not you have found their horses," began the lady, but she was interrupted by Lucy Ann, who entered at the moment with a plate of fresh corn-cakes, and caught the last part of the sentence.

" Come along, Mister," she said, " I 'll show you myself," and she set down her plate, took the candle from the table, and walked to the door, followed by the soldiers.

" Lucy Ann ! " exclaimed her mistress ; but she was too much amazed at the girl's conduct to say more.

" I know whar dey is ! " Lucy Ann continued, taking no notice of her mistress. They heard her say, as she was shutting the door, " Y' all come with me ; I 'feared they gone ; ef they ain't, I know whar they is ! "

" Open every room," said the officer.

" Oh, yes, sir ; I gwine ketch 'em for you," she said, eagerly opening first one door, and then the other, "that is, ef they ain' gone. I mighty 'feared they gone. I seen 'em goin' out the back way about a little while befo' you all come,—but I thought they might 'a' come back. Mister, ken y' all teck me 'long with you when you go ? " she asked the officer, in a low voice. " I want to be free."

"I don't know; we can some other time, if not now. We are going to set you all free."

"Oh, glory! Come 'long, Mister; let's ketch 'em. They ain't heah, but I know whar dey is."

The soldiers closely examined every place where it was possible a man could be concealed, until they had been over all the lower part of the house.

Lucy Ann stopped. "Dey's gone!" she said positively.

The officer motioned to her to go up stairs.

"Yes, sir, I wuz jes' goin' tell you we jes' well look up-stairs, too," she said, leading the way, talking all the time, and shading the flickering candle with her hand.

The little group, flat on the floor against the wall in their dark retreat, could now hear her voice distinctly. She was speaking in a confidential undertone, as if afraid of being overheard.

"I wonder I did n't have sense to get somebody to watch 'em when they went out," they heard her say.

"She 's betrayed us!" whispered Hugh.

The General merely said, "Hush," and laid his hand firmly on the nearest boy to keep him still. Lucy Ann led the soldiers into the various chambers one after another. At last she opened the next room, and, through the wall, the men in hiding heard the soldiers go in and walk about.

They estimated that there were at least half-a-dozen.

"Is n't there a garret?" asked one of the searching party.

" Nor, sir, 't ain't no garret, jes' a loft ; but they ain't up there," said Lucy Ann's voice.

" We 'll look for ourselves." They came out of the room. " Show us the way."

" Look here, if you tell us a lie, we'll hang you ! "

The voice of the officer was very stern.

" I ain' gwine tell you no lie, Mister. What you reckon I wan' tell you lie for ? Dey ain' in the garret, I know,—— Mister, please don't p'int dem things at me. I 's 'feared o' dem things," said the girl in a slightly whimpering voice ; " I gwine show you."

She came straight down the passage toward the recess where the fugitives were huddled, the men after her, their heavy steps echoing through the house. The boys were trembling violently. The light, as the searchers came nearer, fell on the wall, crept along it, until it lighted up the whole alcove, except where they lay. The boys held their breath. They could hear their hearts thumping.

Lucy Ann stepped into the recess with her candle, and looked straight at them.

" They ain't in here," she exclaimed, suddenly putting her hand up before the flame, as if to prevent it flaring, thus throwing the alcove once more into darkness. " The trap-door to the garret 's 'roun' that a-way," she said to the soldiers, still keeping her position at the narrow entrance, as if to let them pass. When they had all passed, she followed them.

The boys began to wriggle with delight, but the General's strong hand kept them still.

Naturally, the search in the garret proved fruitless, and the hiding-party heard the squad swearing over their ill-luck as they came back; while Lucy Ann loudly lamented not having sent some one to follow the fugitives, and made a number of suggestions as to where they had gone, and the probability of catching them if the soldiers went at once in pursuit.

"Did you look in here?" asked a soldier approaching the alcove.

"Yes, sir; they ain't in there." She snuffed the candle out suddenly with her fingers. "Oh, oh!—my light done gone out! Mind! Let me go in front and show you the way," she said; and, pressing before, she once more led them along the passage.

"Mind yo' steps; ken you see?" she asked.

They went down stairs, while Lucy Ann gave them minute directions as to how they might catch "Marse Hugh an' the Gen'l" at a certain place a half-mile from the house (an unoccupied quarter), which she carefully described.

A further investigation ensued downstairs, but in a little while the searchers went out of the house. Their tone had changed since their disappointment, and loud threats floated up the dark stairway to the prisoners still crouching in the little recess.

In a few minutes the boys' Cousin Belle came rushing up stairs.

"Now's your time! Come quick," she called; "they will be back directly. Is n't she an angel!" The whole party sprang to their feet, and ran down to the lower floor.

"Oh, we were so frightened!" "Don't let them see you." "Make haste," were the exclamations that greeted them as the two soldiers said their good-byes and prepared to leave the house.

"Go out by the side-door; that 's your only chance. It 's pitch-dark, and the bushes will hide you. But where are you going?"

"We are going to the boys' cave," said the General, buckling on his pistol; "I know the way, and we 'll get away as soon as these fellows leave, if we cannot before."

"God bless you!" said the ladies, pushing them away in dread of the enemy's return.

"Come on, General," called Hugh in an undertone. The General was lagging behind a minute to say good-bye once more. He stooped suddenly and kissed the boys' Cousin Belle before them all.

"Good-bye. God bless you!" and he followed Hugh out of the window into the darkness. The girl burst into tears and ran up to her room.

A few seconds afterward the house was once more filled with the enemy, growling at their ill-luck in having so narrowly missed the prize.

"We 'll catch 'em yet," said the leader.

CHAPTER XV.

THE raiders were up early next morning scouring the woods and country around. They knew that the fugitive soldiers could not have gone far, for the Federals had every road picketed, and their main body was not far away. As the morning wore on, it became a grave question at Oakland how the two soldiers were to subsist. They had no provisions with them, and the roads were so closely watched that there was no chance of their obtaining any. The matter was talked over, and the boys' mother and Cousin Belle were in despair.

"They can eat their shoes," said Willy, reflectively.

The ladies exclaimed in horror.

"That's what men always do when they get lost in a wilderness where there is no game."

This piece of information from Willy did not impress his hearers as much as he supposed it would.

"I'll tell you! Let me and Frank go and carry 'em something to eat!"

"How do you know where they are?"

"They are at our Robber's Cave, are n't they, Cousin Belle? We told the General yesterday how to get there, did n't we?"

"Yes, and he said last night that he would go there."

Willy's idea seemed a good one, and the offer was accepted. The boys were to go out as if to see the troops, and were to take as much food as they thought could pass for their luncheon. Their mother cooked and put up a luncheon large enough to have satisfied the appetites of two young Brobdingnagians, and they set out on their relief expedition.

The two sturdy little figures looked full of importance as they strode off up the road. They carried many loving messages. Their Cousin Belle gave to each separately a long whispered message which each by himself was to deliver to the General. It was thought best not to hazard a note.

They were watched by the ladies from the portico until they disappeared over the hill. They took a path which led into the woods, and walked cautiously for fear some of the raiders might be lurking about. However, the boys saw none of the enemy, and in a little while they came to a point where the pines began. Then they turned into the woods, for the pines were so thick the boys could not be seen, and the pine tags made it so soft under foot that they could walk without making any noise.

They were pushing their way through the bushes, when Frank suddenly stopped.

"Hush!" he said.

Willy halted and listened.

"There they are."

From a little distance to one side, in the direction of the path they had just left, they heard the trampling of a number of horses' feet.

"That's not our men," said Willy. "Hugh and the General have n't any horses"

"No; that's the Yankees," said Frank. "Let's lie down. They may hear us."

The boys flung themselves upon the ground and almost held their breath until the horses had passed out of hearing.

"Do you reckon they are hunting for us?" asked Willy in an awed whisper.

"No, for Hugh and the General. Come on."

They rose, went tipping a little deeper into the pines, and again made their way toward the cave.

"Maybe they 've caught 'em," suggested Willy.

"They can't catch 'em in these pines," replied Frank. "You can't see any distance at all. A horse can't get through, and the General and Hugh could shoot 'em, and then get away before they could catch 'em."

They hurried on.

"Frank, suppose they take us for Yankees?"

Evidently Willy's mind had been busy since Frank's last speech.

"They are n't going to shoot *us,*" said Frank; but it was an unpleasant suggestion, for they were not very far from the dense clump of pines between two gullies, which the boys called their cave.

"We can whistle," he said, presently.

"Won't Hugh and the General think we are enemies trying to surround them?" Willy objected. The dilemma was a serious one. "We 'll have to crawl up," said Frank after a pause.

And this was agreed upon. They were soon on the edge of the deep gully which, on one side, protected the spot from all approach. They scrambled down its steep side and began to creep along, peeping over its other edge from time to time, to see if they could discover the clearing which marked the little green spot on top of the hill, where once had stood an old cabin. The base of the ruined chimney, with its immense fire-place, constituted the boys' "cave." They were close to it, now, and felt themselves to be in imminent danger of a sweeping fusillade. They had just crept up to the top of the ravine and were consulting, when some one immediately behind them, not twenty feet away, called out:

"Hello! What are you boys doing here? Are you trying to capture us?"

They jumped at the unexpected voice. The General broke into a laugh. He had been sitting on the ground on the other side of the declivity, and had been watching their manœuvres for some time.

He brought them to the house-spot where Hugh was asleep on the ground; he had been on watch all the morning, and, during the General's turn, was making up for his lost sleep. He was soon wide awake enough, and he and the General, with appetites bearing witness to their long fast, were without delay engaged in disposing of the provisions which the boys had brought.

The boys were delighted with the mystery of their surroundings. Each in turn took the General aside and held a long interview with him, and gave him all their Cousin Belle's messages. No one had ever treated them with such consideration as the General showed them. The two men asked the boys all about the dispositions of the enemy, but the boys had little to tell.

"They are after us pretty hotly," said the General. "I think they are going away shortly. It 's nothing but a raid, and they are moving on. We must get back to camp to-night."

"How are you going?" asked the boys. "You have n't any horses."

"We are going to get some of their horses," said the officer. "They have taken ours—now they must furnish us with others."

It was about time for the boys to start for home. The General took each of them aside, and talked for a long time. He was speaking to Willy, on the edge of the clearing, when there was a crack of a twig in the pines. In a second he had laid the boy on his back in the soft grass and whipped out a pistol. Then, with a low, quick call to Hugh, he sprang swiftly into the pines toward the sound.

"Crawl down into the ravine, boys," called Hugh, following his companion. The boys rolled down over the bank like little ground-hogs; but in a second they heard a familiar drawling voice call out in a subdued tone:

"Hold on, Cunnel! it 's nobody but me; don't you know me?" And, in a moment, they heard the General's astonished and somewhat stern reply:

"Mills, what are you doing here? Who 's with you? What do you want?"

"Well," said the new-comer, slowly, "I 'lowed I 'd come to see if I could be o' any use to you. I heard the Yankees had run you 'way from Oakland last night, and was sort o' huntin' for you. Fact is, they 's been up my way, and I sort o' 'lowed I 'd come an' see ef I could help you git back to camp."

"Where have you been all this time? I wonder you are not ashamed to look me in the face!"

The General's voice was still stern. He had turned around and walked back to the cleared space.

The deserter scratched his head in perplexity.

"I need n' 'a' come," he said, doggedly. "Where 's them boys? I don' want the boys hurted. I seen 'em comin' here, an' I jes' followed 'em to see they did n't get in no trouble. But——"

This speech about the boys effected what the offer of personal service to the General himself had failed to bring about.

"Sit down and let me talk to you," said the General, throwing himself on the grass.

Mills seated himself cross-legged near the officer, with his gun across his knees, and began to bite a straw which he pulled from a tuft by his side.

The boys had come up out of their retreat, and taken places on each side of the General.

"You all take to grass like young partridges," said the hunter. The boys were flattered, for they considered any notice from him a compliment.

"What made you fool us, and send us to catch that conscript-guard?" Frank asked.

"Well, you ketched him, did n't you? You 're the only ones ever been able to ketch him," he said, with a low chuckle.

"Now, Mills, you know how things stand," said the General. "It 's a shame for you to have been acting this way. You know what people say about you. But if you come back to camp and do your duty, I 'll have it all straightened out. If you don't, I 'll have you shot."

His voice was as calm and his manner as composed as if he were promising the man opposite him a reward for good conduct. He looked Mills steadily in the eyes all the time. The boys felt as if their friend were about to be executed. The General seemed an immeasurable distance above them.

The deserter blinked twice or thrice, slowly bit his shred of straw, looked casually first toward one boy and then toward the other, but without the slightest change of expression in his face.

8

"Cun'l," he said, at length, "I ain't no deserter. I ain't feared of bein' shot. Ef I was, I would n' 'a' come here now. I 'm gwine wid you, an' I 'm gwine back to my company; an' I 'm gwine fight, ef Yankees gits in my way; but ef I gits tired, I 's comin' home; an' tain't no use to tell you I ain't, 'cause I *is*,—an' ef anybody flings up to me that I 's a-runnin' away, I 'm gwine to kill 'em!"

He rose to his feet in the intensity of his feeling, and his eyes, usually so dull, were like live coals.

The General looked at him quietly a few seconds, then himself arose and laid his hand on Tim Mills' shoulder.

"All right," he said.

"I got a little snack M'lindy put up," said Mills, pulling a substantial bundle out of his game-bag. "I 'lowed maybe you might be sort o' hongry. Jes' two or three squirrels I shot," he said, apologetically.

"You boys better git 'long home, I reckon," said Mills to Willy. "You ain' 'fraid, is you? 'Cause if you is, I 'll go with you."

His voice had resumed its customary drawl.

"Oh, no," said both boys, eagerly. "We are n't afraid."

"An' tell your ma I ain' let nobody tetch nothin' on the Oakland plantation; not sence that day you all went huntin' deserters; not if I knowed 'bout it."

"Yes, sir."

"An' tell her I 'm gwine take good keer o' Hugh an' the Cunnel. Good-bye!—now run along!"

"All right, sir,—good-bye."

"An' ef you hear anybody say Tim Mills is a d'serter, tell 'em it 's a lie, an' you know it. Good-bye." He turned away as if relieved.

The boys said good-bye to all three, and started in the direction of home.

CHAPTER XVI.

AFTER crossing the gully, and walking on through the woods for what they thought a safe distance, they turned into the path.

They were talking very merrily about the General and Hugh and their friend Mills, and were discussing some romantic plan for the recapture of their horses from the enemy, when they came out of the path into the road, and found themselves within twenty yards of a group of Federal soldiers, quietly sitting on their horses, evidently guarding the road.

The sight of the blue-coats made the boys jump. They would have crept back, but it was too late—they caught the eye of the man nearest them. They ceased talking as suddenly as birds in the trees stop chirruping when the hawk sails over; and when one Yankee called to them, in a stern tone, "Halt there!" and started to come toward them, their hearts were in their mouths.

"Where are you boys going?" he asked, as he came up to them.

"Going home."

"Where do you belong?"

"Over there—at Oakland," pointing in the direction of

their home, which seemed suddenly to have moved a thousand miles aways.

"Where have you been?" The other soldiers had come up now.

"Been down this way." The boys' voices were never so meek before. Each reply was like an apology.

"Been to see your brother?" asked one who had not spoken before—a pleasant looking fellow. The boys looked at him. They were paralyzed by dread of the approaching question.

"Now, boys, we know where you have been," said a small fellow, who wore a yellow chevron on his arm. He had a thin moustache and a sharp nose, and rode a wiry, dull sorrel horse. "You may just as well tell us all about it. We know you 've been to see 'em, and we are going to make you carry us where they are."

"No, we ain't," said Frank, doggedly.

Willy expressed his determination also.

"If you don't it 's going to be pretty bad for you," said the little corporal. He gave an order to two of the men, who sprang from their horses, and, catching Frank, swung him up behind another cavalryman. The boy's face was very pale, but he bit his lip.

"Go ahead,"—continued the corporal to a number of his men, who started down the path. "You four men remain here till we come back," he said to the men on the ground, and to two others on horseback. "Keep him here," jerking his thumb toward Willy, whose face was already burning with emotion.

"I 'm going with Frank," said Willy. "Let me go." This to the man who had hold of him by the arm. "Frank, make him let me go," he shouted, bursting into tears, and turning on his captor with all his little might.

"Willy, he 's not goin' to hurt you,—don't you tell!" called Frank, squirming until he dug his heels so into the horse's flanks that the horse began to kick up.

"Keep quiet, Johnny; he 's not goin' to hurt him," said one of the men, kindly. He had a brown beard and shining white teeth.

They rode slowly down the narrow path, the dragoon holding Frank by the leg. Deep down in the woods, beyond a small branch, the path forked.

"Which way?" asked the corporal, stopping and addressing Frank.

Frank set his mouth tight and looked him in the eyes.

"Which is it?" the corporal repeated.

"I ain't going to tell," said he, firmly.

"Look here, Johnny; we 've got you, and we are going to make you tell us; so you might just as well do it, easy. If you don't, we 're goin' to make you."

The boy said nothing.

"You men dismount. Stubbs, hold the horses." He himself dismounted, and three others did the same, giving their horses to a fourth.

THE BOY FACED HIS CAPTOR, WHO HELD A STRAP IN ONE HAND.

"Get down?"—this to Frank and the soldier behind whom he was riding. The soldier dismounted, and the boy slipped off after him and faced his captor, who held a strap in one hand.

"Are you goin' to tell us?" he asked.

"No."

"Don't you know?" He came a step nearer, and held the strap forward. There was a long silence. The boy's face paled perceptibly, but took on a look as if the proceedings were indifferent to him.

"If you say you don't know"—said the man, hesitating in face of the boy's resolution. "Don't you know where they are?"

"Yes, I know; but I ain't goin' to tell you," said Frank, bursting into tears.

"The little Johnny 's game," said the soldier who had told him the others were not going to hurt Willy. The corporal said something to this man in an undertone, to which he replied:

"You can try, but it is n't going to do any good. I don't half like it, anyway."

Frank had stopped crying after his first outburst.

"If you don't tell, we are going to shoot you," said the little soldier, drawing his pistol.

The boy shut his mouth close, and looked straight at the corporal. The man laid down his pistol, and, seizing Frank, drew his hands behind him, and tied them.

"Get ready, men," he said, as he drew the boy aside to a small tree, putting him with his back to it.

Frank thought his hour had come. He thought of his mother and Willy, and wondered if the soldiers would shoot Willy, too. His face twitched and grew ghastly white. Then he thought of his father, and of how proud he would be of his son's bravery when he should hear of it. This gave him strength.

"The knot—hurts my hands," he said.

The man leaned over and eased it a little.

"I was n't crying because I was scared," said Frank.

The kind looking fellow turned away.

"Now, boys, get ready," said the corporal, taking up his pistol.

How large it looked to Frank. He wondered where the bullets would hit him, and if the wounds would bleed, and whether he would be left alone all night out there in the woods, and if his mother would come and kiss him.

"I want to say my prayers," he said, faintly.

The soldier made some reply which he could not hear, and the man with the beard started forward; but just then all grew dark before his eyes.

Next, he thought he must have been shot, for he felt wet about his face, and was lying down. He heard some one say, "He 's coming to;" and another replied, "Thank God!"

He opened his eyes. He was lying beside the little branch with his head in the lap of the big soldier with the beard, and the little corporal was leaning over him throwing water in his face from a cap. The others were standing around.

"What 's the matter?" asked Frank.

"That 's all right," said the little corporal, kindly. "We were just a-foolin' a bit with you, Johnny."

"We never meant to hurt you," said the other. "You feel better now?"

"Yes, where 's Willy?" He was too tired to move.

"He 's all right. We 'll take you to him."

"Am I shot?" asked Frank.

"No! Do you think we 'd have touched a hair of your head—and you such a brave little fellow? We were just trying to scare you a bit and carried it too far, and you got a little faint,—that 's all."

The voice was so kindly that Frank was encouraged to sit up.

"Can you walk now?" asked the corporal, helping him and steadying him as he rose to his feet.

"I 'll take him," said the big fellow, and before the boy could move, he had stooped, taken Frank in his arms, and was carrying him back toward the place where they had left Willy, while the others followed after with the horses.

"I can walk," said Frank.

"No, I 'll carry you, b–bless your heart!"

The boy did not know that the big dragoon was looking down at the light hair resting on his arm, and that while he trod the Virginia wood-path, in fancy he was home in Dela ware; or that the pressure the boy felt from his strong arms was a caress given for the sake of another boy far away on the Brandywine. A little while before they came in sight Frank asked to be put down.

The soldier gently set him on his feet, and before he let him go kissed him.

"I 've got a curly-headed fellow at home, just the size of you," he said softly.

Frank saw that his eyes were moist. "I hope you 'll get safe back to him," he said.

"God grant it!" said the soldier.

When they reached the squad at the gate, they found Willy still in much distress on Frank's account; but he wiped his eyes when his brother reappeared, and listened with pride to the soldiers' praise of Frank's "grit" as they called it. When they let the boys go, the little corporal wished Frank to accept a five-dollar gold piece; but he politely declined it.

CHAPTER XVII.

THE story of Frank's adventure and courage was the talk of all the Oakland plantation. His mother and Cousin Belle both kissed him and called him their little hero. Willy also received a full share of praise for his courage.

About noon there was great commotion among the troops. They were far more numerous than they had been in the morning, and instead of riding about the woods in small bodies, hunting for the concealed soldiers, they were collecting together and preparing to move.

It was learned that a considerable body of cavalry was passing down the road by Trinity Church, and that the depot had been burnt again the night before. Somehow, a rumor got about that the Confederates were following up the raiders.

In an hour most of the soldiers went away, but a number still stayed on. Their horses were picketed about the yard feeding; and they themselves lounged around, making themselves at home in the house, and pulling to pieces the things that were left. They were not, however, as wanton in their destruction as the first set, who had passed by the year before.

Among those who yet remained were the little corporal,

and the big young soldier who had been so kind to Frank. They were in the rear-guard. At length the last man rode off.

The boys had gone in and out among them, without being molested. Now and then some rough fellow would swear at them, but for the most part their intercourse with the boys was friendly. When, therefore, they rode off, the boys were allowed by their mother to go and see the main body.

Peter and Cole were with them. They took the main road and followed along, picking up straps, and cartridges, and all those miscellaneous things dropped by a large body of troops as they pass along.

Cartridges were very valuable, as they furnished the only powder and shot the boys could get for hunting, and their supply was out. These were found in unusual numbers. The boys filled their pockets, and finally filled their sleeves, tying them tightly at the wrist with strings, so that the contents would not spill out. One of the boys found even an old pistol, which was considered a great treasure. He bore it proudly in his belt, and was envied by all the others.

It was quite late in the afternoon when they thought of turning toward home, their pockets and sleeves bagging down with the heavy musket-cartridges. They left the Federal rear-guard feeding their horses at a great white pile of corn which had been thrown out of the corn-house of a neighbor and was scattered all over the ground.

They crossed a field, descended a hill, and took the main

road at its foot, just as a body of cavalry came in sight. A small squad, riding some little distance in advance of the main body, had already passed by. These were Confederates. The first man they saw, at the head of the column by the colonel, was the General, and a little behind him was none other than Hugh on a gray roan; while not far down the column rode their friend Tim Mills, looking rusty and sleepy as usual.

"Goodness! Why here are the General and Hugh! How in the world did you get away?" exclaimed the boys.

They learned that it was a column of cavalry following the line of the raid, and that the General and Hugh had met them and volunteered. The soldiers greeted the boys cordially.

"The Yankees are right up there," said the youngsters.

"Where? How many? What are they doing?" asked the General.

"A whole pack of 'em—right up there at the stables, and all about, feeding their horses and sitting all around, and ever so many more have gone along down the road."

"Fling the fence down there!" The boys pitched down the rails in two or three places. An order was passed back, and in an instant a stir of preparation was noticed all down the line of horsemen.

A courier galloped up the road to recall the advance-guard. The head of the column passed through the gap, and, without waiting for the others, dashed up the hill at a gallop—the General and the colonel a score of yards ahead of any of the others.

"Let's go and see the fight!" cried the boys; and the whole set started back up the hill as fast as their legs could carry them.

"S'pose they shoot! Won't they shoot us?" asked one of the negro boys, in some apprehension. This, though before unthought of, was a possibility, and for a moment brought them down to a slower pace.

"We can lie flat and peep over the top of the hill." This was Frank's happy thought, and the party started ahead again. "Let's go around that way." They made a little detour.

Just before they reached the crest they heard a shot, "bang!" immediately followed by another, "bang!" and in a second more a regular volley began, and was kept up.

They reached the crest of the hill in time to see the Confederates gallop up the slope toward the stables, firing their pistols at the blue-coats, who were forming in the edge of a little wood, over beyond a fence, from the other side of which the smoke of their carbines was rolling. They had evidently started on just as the boys left, and before the Confederates came in sight.

The boys saw their friends dash at this fence, and could distinguish the General and Hugh, who were still in the lead. Their horses took the fence, going over like birds, and others followed,—Tim Mills among them,—while yet more went through a gate a few yards to one side.

"Look at Hugh! Look at Hugh!"

"Look! That horse has fallen down!" cried one of the boys, as a horse went down just at the entrance of the wood, rolling over his rider.

"He's shot!" exclaimed Frank, for neither horse nor rider attempted to rise.

"See; they are running!"

The little squad of blue-coats were retiring into the woods, with the grays closely pressing them.

"Let 's cut across and see 'em run 'em over the bridge."

"Come on!"

All the little group of spectators, white and black, started as hard as they could go for a path they knew, which led by a short cut through the little piece of woods. Beyond lay a field divided by a stream, a short distance on the other side of which was a large body of woods.

The popping was still going on furiously in the woods, and bullets were "zoo-ing" over the fields. But the boys could not see anything, and they did not think about the flying balls.

They were all excitement at the idea of "our men" whipping the enemy, and they ran with all their might to be in time to see them "chase 'em across the field."

The road on which the skirmish took place, and down which the Federal rear-guard had retreated, made a sharp curve beyond the woods, around the bend of a little stream crossed by a small bridge; and the boys, in taking the short

cut, had placed the road between themselves and home; bu
they did not care about that, for their men were driving th
others. They "just wanted to see it."

They reached the edge of the field in time to see tha
the Yankees were on the other side of the stream. The
knew them to be where puffs of smoke came out of the oppo
site wood. And the Confederates had stopped beyond th
bridge, and were halted, in some confusion, in the field.

The firing was very sharp, and bullets were singing i
every direction. Then the Confederates got together, an
went as hard as they could right at them up to the wood, al
along the edge of which the smoke was pouring in continuou
puffs and with a rattle of shots. They saw several horses fal
as the Confederates galloped on, but the smoke hid most o
it. Next they saw a long line of fire appear in the smoke or
both sides of the road, where it entered the wood; then the
Confederates stopped, and became all mixed up; a number o
horses galloped away without their riders, another line o
white and red flame came out of the woods, the Confederates began to come back, leaving many horses on the ground
and a body of cavalry in blue coats poured out of the wood
in pursuit.

"Look! look! They are running—they are beating our
men!" exclaimed the boys. "They have driven 'em back
across the bridge!"

"How many of them there are!"

"What shall we do? Suppose they see us!"

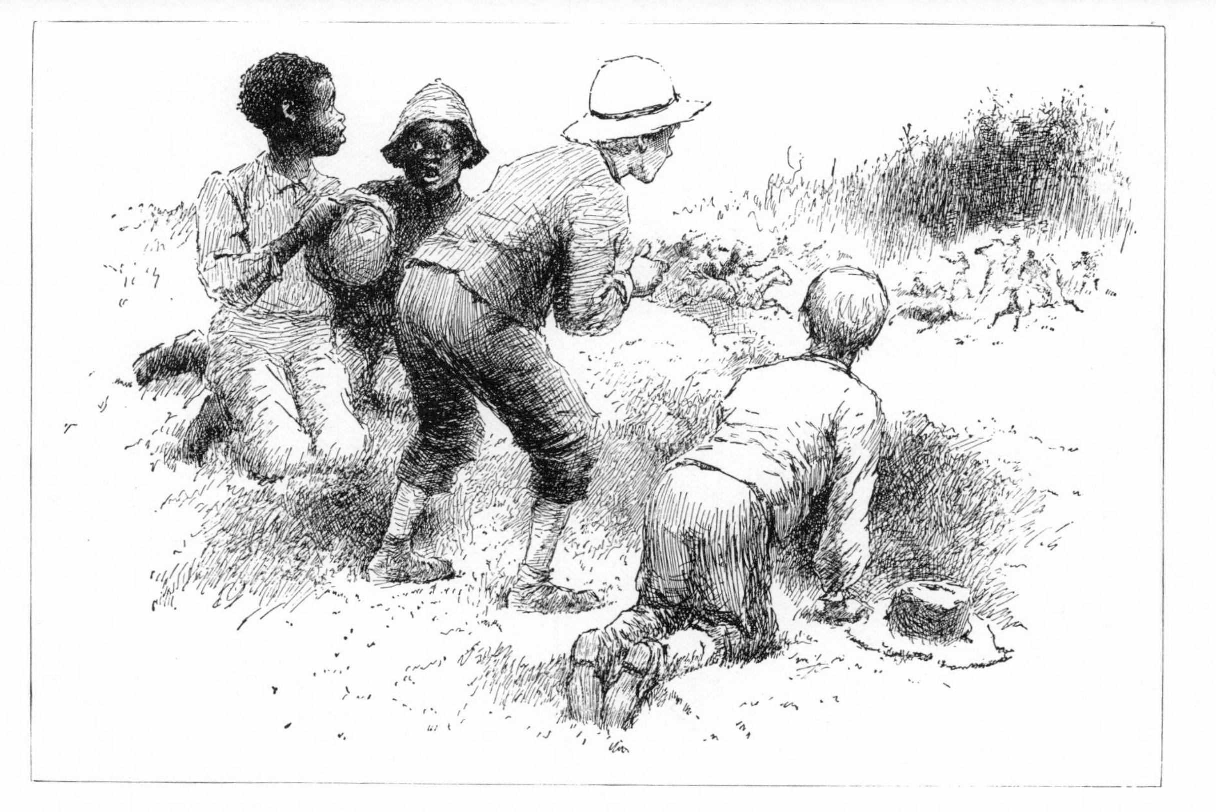

"LOOK! LOOK! THEY ARE RUNNING! THEY ARE BEATING OUR MEN!" EXCLAIMED THE BOYS.

"Come on, Mah'srs Frank 'n' Willy, let 's go home," said
he colored boys. "They 'll shoot us."

The fight was now in the woods which lay between the
oys and their home. But just then the gray-coats got
ogether, again turned at the edge of the wood, and dashed
ack on their pursuers, and—the smoke and bushes on the
tream hid everything. In a second more both emerged on
he other side of the smoke and went into the woods on the
urther edge of the field, all in confusion, and leaving on the
ground more horses and men than before.

"What 's them things 'zip-zippin' 'round my ears?" asked
one of the negro boys.

"Bullets," said Frank, proud of his knowledge.

"Will they hurt me if they hit me?"

"Of course they will. They 'll kill you."

"I 'm gwine home," said the boy, and off he started at a
rot.

"Hold on!—We 're goin', too; but let 's go down this
way; this is the best way."

They went along the edge of the field, toward the point
n the road where the skirmish had been and where the Confederates had rallied. They stopped to listen to the popping
in the woods on the other side, and were just saying how glad
they were that "our men had whipped them," when a soldier
came along.

"What in the name of goodness are you boys doing
here?" he asked.

"We 're just looking on an' lis'ning," answered the boys meekly.

"Well, you 'd better be getting home as fast as you can. They are too strong for us, and they 'll be driving us back directly, and some of you may get killed or run over."

This was dreadful! Such an idea had never occurred to the boys. A panic took possession of them.

"Come on! Let 's go home!" This was the universal idea, and in a second the whole party were cutting straight for home, utterly stampeded.

They could readily have found shelter and security back over the hill, from the flying balls; but they preferred to get home, and they made straight for it. The popping of the guns, which still kept up in the woods across the little river, now meant to them that the victorious Yankees were driving back their friends. They believed that the bullets which now and then yet whistled over the woods with a long, singing "zoo-ee," were aimed at them. For their lives, then, they ran, expecting to be killed every minute.

The load of cartridges in their pockets, which they had carried for hours, weighed them down. As they ran they threw these out. Then followed those in their sleeves. Frank and the other boys easily got rid of theirs, but Willy had tied the strings around his wrists in such hard knots that he could not possibly untie them. He was falling behind.

Frank heard him call. Without slacking his speed he

looked back over his shoulder. Willy's face was red, and his mouth was twitching. He was sobbing a little, and was tearing at the strings with his teeth as he ran. Then the strings came loose one after the other, the cartridges were shaken out over the ground, and Willy's face at once cleared up as he ran forward lightened of his load.

They had passed almost through the narrow skirt of woods where the first attack was made, when they heard some one not far from the side of the road call, "Water!"

The boys stopped. "What 's that?" they asked each other in a startled undertone. A groan came from the same direction, and a voice said, "Oh, for some water!"

A short, whispered consultation was held.

"He 's right up on that bank. There 's a road up there."

Frank advanced a little; a man was lying somewhat propped up against a tree. His eyes were closed, and there was a ghastly wound in his head.

"Willy, it 's a Yankee, and he 's shot."

"Is he dead?" asked the others, in awed voices.

"No. Let 's ask him if he 's hurt much."

They all approached him. His eyes were shut and his face was ashy white.

"Willy, it 's *my* Yankee!" exclaimed Frank.

The wounded man moved his hand at the sound of the voices.

"Water," he murmured. "Bring me water, for pity's sake!"

"I 'll get you some,—don't you know me? Let me have your canteen," said Frank, stooping and taking hold of the canteen. It was held by its strap; but the boy whipped out a knife and cut it loose.

The man tried to speak; but the boys could not understand him.

"Where are you goin' get it, Frank?" asked the other boys.

"At the branch down there that runs into the creek."

"The Yankees 'll shoot you down there," objected Peter and Willy.

"*I* ain' gwine that way," said Cole.

The soldier groaned.

"*I'll* go with you, Frank," said Willy, who could not stand the sight of the man's suffering.

"We 'll be back directly."

The two boys darted off, the others following them at a little distance. They reached the open field. The shooting was still going on in the woods on the other side, but they no longer thought of it. They ran down the hill and dashed across the little flat to the branch at the nearest point, washed the blood from the canteen, and filled it with the cool water.

"I wish we had something to wash his face with," sighed Willy, "but I have n't got a handkerchief."

"Neither have I." Willy looked thoughtful. A second more and he had stripped off his light sailor's jacket and dipped it in the water. The next minute the two boys were running up the hill again.

When they reached the spot where the wounded man lay, he had slipped down and was flat on the ground. His feeble voice still called for water, but was much weaker than before. Frank stooped and held the canteen to the man's lips, and he drank. Then Willy and Frank, together, bathed his face with the still dripping cotton jacket. This revived him somewhat; but he did not recognize them and talked incoherently. They propped up his head.

"Frank, it's getting mighty late, and we've got to go home," said Willy.

The boys' voice or words reached the ears of the wounded man.

"Take me home," he murmured; "I want some water from the well by the dairy."

"Give him some more water."

Willy lifted the canteen. "Here it is."

The soldier swallowed with difficulty.

He could not raise his hand now. There was a pause. The boys stood around, looking down on him. "I've come back home," he said. His eyes were closed.

"He's dreaming," whispered Willy.

"Did you ever see anybody die?" asked Frank, in a low tone.

Willy's face paled.

"No, Frank; let's go home and tell somebody."

Frank stooped and touched the soldier's face. He was talking all the time now, though they could not understand everything he said. The boy's touch seemed to rouse him.

"It 's bedtime," he said, presently. "Kneel down and say your prayers for Father."

"Willy, let 's say our prayers for him," whispered Frank.

"I can say, 'Now I lay me.'" But before he could begin,

"'Now I lay me down to sleep,'" said the soldier tenderly. The boys followed him, thinking he had heard them. They did not know that he was saying—for one whom but that morning he had called "his curly-head at home"—the prayer that is common to Virginia and to Delaware, to North and to South, and which no wars can silence and no victories cause to be forgotten.

The soldier's voice now was growing almost inaudible. He spoke between long-drawn breaths.

"'If I should die before I wake.'"

"'If I should die before I wake,'" they repeated, and continued the prayer.

"'And this I ask for Jesus' sake,'" said the boys, ending. There was a long pause. Frank stroked the pale face softly with his hand.

"'And this I ask for Jesus' sake,'" whispered the lips. Then, very softly, "Kiss me good-night."

"Kiss him, Frank."

The boy stooped over and kissed the lips that had kissed

him in the morning. Willy kissed him, also. The lips moved in a faint smile.

"God bless——"

The boys waited,—but that was all. The dusk settled down in the woods. The prayer was ended.

"He 's dead," said Frank, in deep awe.

"Frank, are n't you mighty sorry?" asked Willy in a trembling voice. Then he suddenly broke out crying.

"I don't want him to die! I don't want him to die!"

CHAPTER XVIII.

WHEN the boys reached home it was pitch-dark. They found their mother very anxious about them. They gave an account of the "battle," as they called it, telling all about the charge, in which, by their statement, the General and Hugh did wonderful deeds. Their mother and Cousin Belle sat and listened with tightly folded hands and blanched faces.

Then they told how they found the wounded Yankee soldier on the bank, and about his death. They were startled by seeing their Cousin Belle suddenly fall on her knees and throw herself across their mother's lap in a passion of tears. Their mother put her arms around the young girl, kissed and soothed her.

Early the next morning their mother had an ox-cart (the only vehicle left on the place,) sent down to the spot to bring the body of the soldier up to Oakland, so that it might be buried in the grave-yard there. Carpenter William made the coffin, and several men were set to work to dig the grave in the garden.

It was about the middle of the day when the cart came back. A sheet covered the body. The little cortege was a very solemn one, the steers pulling slowly up the hill and a man walking on each side. Then the body was put into the coffin and reverently carried to the grave. The boys' mother read the burial service out of the prayer-book, and afterward Uncle William Slow offered a prayer. Just as they were about to turn away, the boys' mother began to sing, "Abide with me; fast falls the eventide." She and Cousin Belle and the boys sang the hymn together, and then all walked sadly away, leaving the fresh mound in the garden, where birds peeped curiously from the lilac-bushes at the soldier's grave in the warm light of the afternoon sun.

A small packet of letters and a gold watch and chain, found in the soldier's pocket, were sealed up by the boys' mother and put in her bureau drawer, for they could not then be sent through the lines. There was one letter, however, which they buried with him. It contained two locks of hair, one gray, the other brown and curly.

The next few months brought no new incidents, but the following year deep gloom fell upon Oakland. It was not only that the times were harder than they had ever been—though the plantation was now utterly destitute; there were no provisions and no crops, for there were no teams. It was not merely that a shadow was settling down on all the land; for the boys did not trouble themselves about these things, though such anxieties were bringing gray hairs to their mother's temples.

The General had been wounded and captured during a cavalry-fight. The boys somehow connected their Cousin

Belle with the General's capture, and looked on her with some disfavor. She and the General had quarrelled a short time before, and it was known that she had returned his ring. When, therefore, he was shot through the body and taken by the enemy, the boys could not admit that their cousin had any right to stay up-stairs in her own room weeping about it. They felt that it was all her own fault, and they told her so; whereupon she simply burst out crying and ran from the room.

The hard times grew harder. The shadow deepened. Hugh was wounded and captured in a charge at Petersburg, and it was not known whether he was badly hurt or not. Then came the news that Richmond had been evacuated. The boys knew that this was a defeat; but even then they did not believe that the Confederates were beaten. Their mother was deeply affected by the news.

That night at least a dozen of the negroes disappeared. The other servants said the missing ones had gone to Richmond "to get their papers."

A week or so later the boys heard the rumor that General Lee had surrendered at a place called Appomattox. When they came home and told their mother what they had heard, she turned as pale as death, arose, and went into her chamber. The news was corroborated next day. During the following two days, every negro on the plantation left, excepting lame old Sukey Brown. Some of them came and said they had to go to Richmond, that "the word had come" for them.

Others, including even Uncle Balla and Lucy Ann, slipped away by night.

After that their mother had to cook, and the boys milked and did the heavier work. The cooking was not much trouble, however, for black-eyed pease were about all they had to eat.

One afternoon, the second day after the news of Lee's surrender, the boys, who had gone to drive up the cows to be milked, saw two horsemen, one behind the other, coming slowly down the road on the far hill. The front horse was white, and, as their father rode a white horse, they ran toward the house to carry the news. Their mother and Cousin Belle, however, having seen the horsemen, were waiting on the porch as the men came through the middle gate and rode across the field.

It was their father and his body-servant, Ralph, who had been with him all through the war. They came slowly up the hill; the horses limping and fagged, the riders dusty and drooping.

It seemed like a funeral. The boys were near the steps, and their mother stood on the portico with her forehead resting against a pillar. No word was spoken. Into the yard they rode at a walk, and up to the porch. Then their father, who had not once looked up, put both hands to his face, slipped from his horse, and walked up the steps, tears running down his cheeks, and took their mother into his arms. It *was* a funeral—the Confederacy was dead.

A little later, their father, who had been in the house, came out on the porch near where Ralph still stood holding the horses.

"Take off the saddles, Ralph, and turn the horses out," he said.

Ralph did so.

"Here,—here 's my last dollar. You have been a faithful servant to me. Put the saddles on the porch." It was done. "You are free," he said to the black, and then he walked back into the house.

Ralph stood where he was for some minutes without moving a muscle. His eyes blinked mechanically. Then he looked at the door and at the windows above him. Suddenly he seemed to come to himself. Turning slowly, he walked solemnly out of the yard.

CHAPTER XIX.

THE boys' Uncle William came the next day. The two weeks which followed were the hardest the boys had ever known. As yet nothing had been heard of Hugh or the General, though the boys' father went to Richmond to see whether they had been released.

The family lived on corn-bread and black-eyed pease. There was not a mouthful of meat on the plantation. A few aged animals were all that remained on the place.

The boys' mother bought a little sugar and made some cakes, and the boys, day after day, carried them over to the depot and left them with a man there to be sold. Such a thing had never been known before in the history of the family.

A company of Yankees were camped very near, but they did not interfere with the boys. They bought the cakes and paid for them in greenbacks, which were the first new money they had at Oakland. One day the boys were walking along the road, coming back from the camp, when they met a little old one-horse wagon driven by a man who lived near the depot. In it were a boy about Willy's size and an old lady with white hair, both in deep mourning. The boy was better dressed than any boy they had ever seen. They were strangers.

The boys touched their limp little hats to the lady, and felt somewhat ashamed of their own patched clothes in the presence of the well-dressed stranger. Frank and Willy passed on. They happened to look back. The wagon stopped just then, and the lady called them:

"Little boys!"

They halted and returned.

"We are looking for my son; and this gentleman tells me that you live about here, and know more of the country than any one else I may meet."

"Do you know where any graves is?—Yankee graves?" asked the driver, cutting matters short.

"Yes, there are several down on the road by Pigeon Hill, where the battle was, and two or three by the creek down yonder, and there 's one in our garden."

"Where was your son killed, ma'am? Do you know that he was killed?" asked the driver.

"I do not know. We fear that he was; but, of course, we still hope there may have been some mistake. The last seen of him was when General Sheridan went through this country, last year. He was with his company in the rear-guard, and was wounded and left on the field. We hoped he might have been found in one of the prisons; but there is no trace of him, and we fear——"

She broke down and began to cry. "He was my only son," she sobbed, "my only son—and I gave him up for the Union, and——" She could say no more.

THE BOYS SELL THEIR CAKES TO THE YANKEES.

Her distress affected the boys deeply.

"If I could but find his grave. Even that would be better than this agonizing suspense."

"What was your son's name?" asked the boys, gently.

She told them.

"Why, that's our soldier!" exclaimed both boys.

"Do you know him?" she asked eagerly. "Is—? Is—?" Her voice refused to frame the fearful question.

"Yes, 'm. In our garden," said the boys, almost inaudibly.

The mother bent her head over on her grandson's shoulder and wept aloud. Awful as the suspense had been, now that the last hope was removed the shock was terrible. She gave a stifled cry, then wept with uncontrollable grief.

The boys, with pale faces and eyes moist with sympathy, turned away their heads and stood silent. At length she grew calmer.

"Won't you come home with us? Our father and mother will be so glad to have you," they said, hospitably.

After questioning them a little further, she decided to go. The boys climbed into the back of the wagon. As they went along, the boys told her all about her son,—his carrying Frank, their finding him wounded near the road, and about his death and burial.

"He was a real brave soldier," they told her consolingly.

As they approached the house, she asked whether they could give her grandson something to eat.

"Oh, yes, indeed. Certainly," they answered. Then, thinking perhaps they were raising her hopes too high, they explained apologetically:

"We have n't got much. We did n't kill any squirrels this morning. Both our guns are broken and don't shoot very well, now."

She was much impressed by the appearance of the place, which looked very beautiful among the trees.

"Oh, yes, they're big folks," said the driver.

She would have waited at the gate when they reached the house, but the boys insisted that they all should come in at once. One of them ran forward and, meeting his mother just coming out to the porch, told who the visitor was.

Their mother instantly came down the steps and walked toward the gate. The women met face to face. There was no introduction. None was needed.

"My son—" faltered the elder lady, her strength giving out.

The boy's mother put her handkerchief to her eyes.

"I have one, too;—God alone knows where he is," she sobbed.

Each knew how great was the other's loss, and in sympathy with another's grief found consolation for her own.

CHAPTER XX.

THE visitors remained at Oakland for several days, as the lady wished to have her son's remains removed to the old homestead in Delaware. She was greatly distressed over the want which she saw at Oakland—for there was literally nothing to eat but black-eyed pease and the boys' chickens. Every incident of the war interested her. She was delighted with their Cousin Belle, and took much interest in her story, which was told by the boys' mother.

Her grandson, Dupont, was a fine, brave, and generous young fellow. He had spent his boyhood near a town, and could neither ride, swim, nor shoot as the Oakland boys did; but he was never afraid to try anything, and the boys took a great liking to him, and he to them.

When the young soldier's body had been removed, the visitors left; not, however, until the boys had made their companion promise to pay them a visit. After the departure of these friends they were much missed.

But the next day there was a great rejoicing at Oakland. Every one was in the dining-room at dinner, and the boys' father had just risen from the table and walked out of the room. A second later they heard an exclamation of astonishment from him, and he called eagerly to his wife, "Come here, quickly!" and ran down the steps. Every one rose and ran out. Hugh and the General were just entering the yard.

They were pale and thin and looked ill; but all the past was forgotten in the greeting.

The boys soon knew that the General was making his peace with their Cousin Belle, who looked prettier than ever. It required several long walks before all was made right; but there was no disposition toward severity on either side. It was determined that the wedding was to take place very soon. The boys' father suggested, as an objection to an immediate wedding, that since the General was just half his usual size, it would be better to wait until he should regain his former proportions, so that all of him might be married; but the General would not accept the proposition for delay, and Cousin Belle finally consented to be married at once.

The old place was in a great stir over the preparations. A number of the old servants, including Uncle Balla and Lucy Ann, had one by one come back to their old home. The trunks in the garret were ransacked once more, and enough was found to make up a wedding trousseau of two dresses.

Hugh was to be the General's best man, and the boys were to be the ushers. The only difficulty was that their patched clothes made them feel a little abashed at the prominent rôles they were to assume. However, their mother

SOME OF THE SERVANTS CAME BACK TO THEIR OLD HOME.

made them each a nice jacket from a striped dress, one of her only two dresses, and she adorned them with the military brass buttons their father had had taken from his coat; so they felt very proud. Their father, of course, was to give the bride away,—an office he accepted with pleasure, he said, provided he did not have to move too far, which might be hazardous so long as he had to wear his spurs to keep the soles on his boots.

Thus, even amid the ruins, the boys found life joyous, and if they were without everything else, they had life, health, and hope. The old guns were broken, and they had to ride in the ox-cart; but they hoped to have others and to do better, some day.

The "some day" came sooner than they expected.

The morning before the wedding, word came that there were at the railroad station several boxes for their mother. The ox-cart was sent for them. When the boxes arrived, that evening, there was a letter from their friend in Delaware, congratulating Cousin Belle and apologizing for having sent "a few things" to her Southern friends.

The "few things" consisted not only of necessaries, but of everything which good taste could suggest. There was a complete trousseau for Cousin Belle, and clothes for each member of the family. The boys had new suits of fine cloth with shirts and underclothes in plenty.

But the best surprise of all was found when they came to

the bottom of the biggest box, and found two long, narrow cases, marked, "For the Oakland boys." These cases held beautiful, new double-barreled guns of the finest make. There was a large supply of ammunition, and in each case there was a letter from Dupont promising to come and spend his vacation with them, and sending his love and good wishes and thanks to his friends—the "Two Little Confederates."

THE END.

THE LITTLE COLONEL

"*Cosy Corner Series*"

THE LITTLE COLONEL

BY

ANNIE FELLOWS-JOHNSTON

AUTHOR OF "BIG BROTHER"

Illustrated by Etheldred B. Barry

BOSTON
JOSEPH KNIGHT COMPANY
1896

TO ONE OF
KENTUCKY'S DEAREST LITTLE DAUGHTERS
"THE LITTLE COLONEL" HERSELF—
THIS REMEMBRANCE OF A HAPPY SUMMER
IS AFFECTIONATELY INSCRIBED

ILLUSTRATIONS

THE LITTLE COLONEL.

CHAPTER I.

It was one of the prettiest places in all Kentucky where the Little Colonel stood that morning. She was reaching up on tiptoes, her eager little face pressed close against the iron bars of the great entrance gate that led to a fine old estate known as "Locust."

A ragged little Scotch and Skye terrier stood on its hind feet beside her, thrusting his inquisitive nose between the bars, and wagging his tasselled tail in lively approval of the scene before them.

They were looking down a long avenue that stretched for nearly a quarter of a mile between rows of stately old locust trees.

At the far end they could see the white pillars of a large stone house gleaming through the Virginia creeper that nearly covered it. But they could not see the old Colonel in his big chair on the porch behind the cool screen of vines.

At that very moment he had caught the rattle

of wheels along the road, and had picked up his field glass to see who was passing. It was only a colored man jogging along in the heat and dust with a cart full of chicken coops. The Colonel watched him drive up a lane that led to the back of the new hotel that had just been opened in this quiet country place. Then his glance fell on the two small strangers coming through his gate down the avenue toward him. One was the friskiest dog he had ever seen in his life. The other was a child he judged to be about five years old.

Her shoes were covered with dust, and her white sunbonnet had slipped off and was hanging over her shoulders. A bunch of wild flowers she had gathered on the way hung limp and faded in her little warm hand. Her soft, light hair was cut as short as a boy's.

There was something strangely familiar about the child, especially in the erect, graceful way she walked.

Old Colonel Lloyd was puzzled. He had lived all his life in Lloydsborough, and this was the first time he had ever failed to recognize one of the neighbors' children. He knew every dog and horse too, by sight if not by name.

Living so far back from the public road did not limit his knowledge of what was going on in the world. A powerful field glass brought every passing object in plain view, while he was saved all annoyance of noise and dust.

"I ought to know that child as well as I know my own name," he said to himself. "But the dog is a stranger in these parts. Liveliest thing I ever set eyes on! They must have come from the hotel. Wonder what they want."

He carefully wiped the lens for a better view. When he looked again he saw that they evidently had not come to visit him.

They had stopped half way down the avenue, and climbed up on a rustic seat to rest.

The dog sat motionless about two minutes, his red tongue hanging out as if he were completely exhausted.

Suddenly he gave a spring, and bounded away through the tall blue grass. He was back again in a moment, with a stick in his mouth. Standing up with his fore paws in the lap of his little mistress, he looked so wistfully into her face that she could not refuse this invitation for a romp.

The Colonel chuckled as they went tumbling about in the grass to find the stick which the child repeatedly tossed away.

He hitched his chair along to the other end of the porch as they kept getting farther away from the avenue.

It had been many a long year since those old locust trees had seen a sight like that. Children never played any more under their dignified shadows.

Time had been (but they only whispered this among themselves on rare spring days like this) when the little feet chased each other up and down the long walk, as much at home as the pewees in the beeches.

Suddenly the little maid stood up straight, and began to sniff the air, as if some delicious odor had blown across the lawn.

"Fritz," she exclaimed in delight, "I 'mell 'trawberries!"

The Colonel, who could not hear the remark, wondered at the abrupt pause in the game. He understood it, however, when he saw them wading through the tall grass, straight to his strawberry bed. It was the pride of his heart, and the finest for miles around. The first berries of the season had been picked only the day before. Those that now hung temptingly red on the vines he intended to send to his next neighbor, to prove his boasted claim of always raising the finest and earliest fruit.

He did not propose to have his plans spoiled by these stray guests. Laying the field glass in its accustomed place on the little table beside his chair, he picked up his hat and strode down the walk.

Colonel Lloyd's friends all said he looked like Napoleon, or rather like Napoleon might have looked had he been born and bred a Kentuckian.

He made an imposing figure in his suit of white duck.

The Colonel always wore white from May till October.

There was a military precision about him, from his erect carriage to the cut of the little white goatee on his determined chin.

No one looking into the firm lines of his resolute face could imagine him ever abandoning a purpose or being turned aside when he once formed an opinion.

Most children were afraid of him. The darkies about the place shook in their shoes when he frowned. They had learned from experience that " ole Marse Lloyd had a tigah of a tempah in him."

As he passed down the walk there were two mute witnesses to his old soldier life. A spur gleamed on his boot heel, for he had just returned from his morning ride, and his right sleeve hung empty.

He had won his title bravely. He had given his only son and his strong right arm to the

Southern cause. That had been nearly thirty years ago.

He did not charge down on the enemy with his usual force this time. The little head, gleaming like sunshine in the strawberry patch, reminded him so strongly of a little fellow who used to follow him everywhere, — Tom, the sturdiest, handsomest boy in the county, — Tom, whom he had been so proud of, whom he had so nearly worshipped.

Looking at this fair head bent over the vines, he could almost forget that Tom had ever outgrown his babyhood, that he had shouldered a rifle and followed him to camp, a mere boy, to be shot down by a Yankee bullet in his first battle.

The old Colonel could almost believe he had him back again, and that he stood in the midst of those old days the locusts sometimes whispered about.

He could not hear the happiest of little voices that was just then saying, "Oh, Fritz, isn't you glad we came? An' isn't you glad we've got a gran'fathah with such good 'trawberries?"

It was hard for her to put the *s* before her consonants.

As the Colonel came nearer she tossed another berry into the dog's mouth. A twig snapped, and she raised a startled face toward him.

"Suh ?" she said timidly, for it seemed to her that the stern, piercing eyes had spoken.

"What are you doing here, child?" he asked in a voice so much kinder than his eyes that she regained her usual self-possession at once.

"Eatin' 'trawberries," she answered coolly.

"Who are you, anyway ?" he exclaimed, much puzzled. As he asked the question his gaze happened to rest on the dog, who was peering at him through the ragged, elfish wisps of hair nearly covering its face, with eyes that were startlingly human.

"'Peak when yo'ah 'poken to, Fritz," she said severely, at the same time popping another luscious berry into her mouth.

Fritz obediently gave a long yelp. The Colonel smiled grimly.

"What's *your* name?" he asked, this time looking directly at her.

"Mothah calls me her baby," was the soft-spoken reply, "but papa an' Mom Beck they calls me the Little Cun'l."

"What under the sun do they call you that for ?" he roared.

"'Cause I'm so much like you," was the startling answer.

"Like me!" fairly gasped the Colonel. "How are you like me?"

"Oh, I'm got such a vile tempah, an' I stamps my foot when I gets mad, an' gets all

red in the face. An' I hollahs at folks, an' looks jus' zis way."

She drew her face down and puckered her lips into such a sullen pout that it looked as if a thunder-storm had passed over it. The next instant she smiled up at him serenely.

The Colonel laughed. "What makes you think I am like that?" he said. "You never saw me before."

"Yes, I have too," she persisted. "You's a-hangin' in a gold frame over ou' mantel."

Just then a clear, high voice was heard calling out in the road.

The child started up in alarm. "Oh deah," she exclaimed in dismay, at sight of the stains on her white dress, where she had been kneeling on the fruit, "that's Mom Beck. Now I'll be tied up, and maybe put to bed for runnin' away again. But the berries is mighty nice," she added politely. "Good mawnin', suh. Fritz, we mus' be goin' now."

The voice was coming nearer.

"I'll walk down to the gate with you," said the Colonel, anxious to learn something more about his little guest.

"Oh, you'd bettah not, suh!" she cried in alarm. "Mom Beck doesn't like you a bit. She just hates you! She's goin' to give you a piece of her mind the next time she sees you. I heard her tell Aunt Nervy so."

There was as much real distress in the child's voice as if she were telling him of a promised flogging.

"Lloyd! Aw Lloy-eed!" the call came again.

A neat-looking colored woman glanced in at the gate as she was passing by, and then stood still in amazement. She had often found her little charge playing along the roadside or hiding behind trees, but she had never before known her to pass through any one's gate.

As the name came floating down to him through the clear air, a change came over the Colonel's stern face. He stooped over the child. His hand trembled as he put it under her soft chin and raised her eyes to his.

"Lloyd, Lloyd!" he repeated in a puzzled way. "Can it be possible? There certainly is a wonderful resemblance. You have my little Tom's hair, and only my baby Elizabeth ever had such hazel eyes."

He caught her up in his one arm, and strode on to the gate, where the colored woman stood.

"Why, Becky, is that you?" he cried, recognizing an old trusted servant who had lived at Locust in his wife's lifetime.

Her only answer was a sullen nod.

"Whose child is this?" he asked eagerly, without seeming to notice her defiant looks. "Tell me if you can."

"How can I tell you, suh," she demanded indignantly, "when you have fo'bidden even her name to be spoken befo' you?"

A harsh look came into the Colonel's eyes. He put the child hastily down, and pressed his lips together.

"Don't tie my sunbonnet, Mom Beck," she

begged. Then she waved her hand with an engaging smile.

"Good by, suh," she said graciously. "We've had a mighty nice time!"

The Colonel took off his hat with his usual courtly bow, but he spoke no word in reply.

When the last flutter of her dress had disappeared around the bend of the road, he walked slowly back toward the house.

Halfway down the long avenue where she had stopped to rest, he sat down on the same rustic seat. He could feel her soft little fingers resting on his neck, where they had lain when he carried her to the gate.

A very un-Napoleon-like mist blurred his sight for a moment. It had been so long since such a touch had thrilled him, so long since any caress had been given him.

More than a score of years had gone by since Tom had been laid in a soldier's grave, and the years that Elizabeth had been lost to him seemed almost a lifetime.

And this was Elizabeth's little daughter. Something very warm and sweet seemed to surge across his heart as he thought of the Little Colonel. He was glad, for a moment, that they called her that; glad that his only grandchild looked enough like himself for others to see the resemblance.

But the feeling passed as he remembered that his daughter had married against his wishes, and he had closed his doors forever against her.

The old bitterness came back redoubled in its force.

The next instant he was stamping down the avenue, roaring for Walker, his body-servant, in such a tone that the cook's advice was speedily taken: "Bettah hump yo'self outen dis heah kitchen befo' de ole tigah gits to lashin' roun' any pearter."

CHAPTER II.

Mom Beck carried the ironing-board out of the hot kitchen, set the irons off the stove, and then tiptoed out to the side porch of the little cottage.

"Is yo' head feelin' any bettah, honey?" she said to the pretty, girlish-looking woman lying in the hammock. "I promised to step up to the hotel this evenin' to see one of the chambah-maids. I thought I'd take the Little Cun'l along with me if you was willin'. She's always wild to play with Mrs. Wyford's children up there."

"Yes, I'm better, Becky," was the languid reply. "Put a clean dress on Lloyd if you are going to take her out."

Mrs. Sherman closed her eyes again, thinking gratefully, "Dear, faithful old Becky! What a comfort she has been all my life, first as my nurse, and now as Lloyd's! She is worth her weight in gold!"

The afternoon shadows were stretching long across the grass when Mom Beck led the child up the green slope in front of the hotel.

The Little Colonel had danced along so gayly

with Fritz that her cheeks glowed like wild roses. She made a quaint little picture with such short sunny hair and dark eyes shining out from under the broad-brimmed white hat she wore.

Several ladies who were sitting on the shady piazza, busy with their embroidery, noticed her admiringly.

"It's Elizabeth Lloyd's little daughter," one of them explained. "Don't you remember what a scene there was some years ago when she married a New York man? Sherman, I believe, his name was, Jack Sherman. He was a splendid fellow, and enormously wealthy. Nobody could say a word against him, except that he was a Northerner. That was enough for the old Colonel, though. He hates Yankees like poison. He stormed and swore, and forbade Elizabeth ever coming in his sight again. He had her room locked up, and not a soul on the place ever dares mention her name in his hearing."

The Little Colonel sat down demurely on the piazza steps to wait for the children. The nurse had not finished dressing them for the evening.

She amused herself by showing Fritz the pictures in an illustrated weekly. It was not long until she began to feel that the ladies were talking about her. She had lived among older people so entirely that her thoughts were much deeper than her baby speeches would lead one to suppose.

She understood dimly, from what she had heard the servants say, that there was some trouble between her mother and grandfather. Now she heard it rehearsed from beginning to end. She could not understand what they meant by "bank failures" and "unfortunate investments," but she understood enough to know that her father had lost nearly all his money, and had gone west to make more.

Mrs. Sherman had moved from their elegant New York home two weeks ago to this little cottage in Lloydsborough that her mother had left her. Instead of the houseful of servants they used to have, there was only faithful Mom Beck to do everything.

There was something magnetic in the child's eyes.

Mrs. Wyford shrugged her shoulders uneasily as she caught their piercing gaze fixed on her.

"I do believe that little witch understood every word I said," she exclaimed.

"Oh, certainly not," was the reassuring answer. "She's such a little thing."

But she had heard it all, and understood enough to make her vaguely unhappy. Going home she did not frisk along with Fritz, but walked soberly by Mom Beck's side, holding tight to the friendly black hand.

"We'll go through the woods," said Mom Beck, lifting her over the fence. "It's not so long that way."

As they followed the narrow, straggling path into the cool dusk of the woods, she began to sing. The crooning chant was as mournful as a funeral dirge.

"The clouds hang heavy, an' it's gwine to rain.
Fa'well, my dyin' friends.
I'm gwine to lie in the silent tomb.
Fa'well, my dyin' friends."

A muffled little sob made her stop and look down in surprise.

"Why, what's the mattah, honey?" she exclaimed. "Did Emma Louise make you mad? Or is you cryin' 'cause you're so ti'ed? Come! Ole Becky'll tote her baby the rest of the way."

She picked the light form up in her arms, and pressing the troubled little face against her shoulder, resumed her walk and her song.

"It's a world of trouble we're travellin' through.
Fa'well, my dyin' friends."

"Oh, don't, Mom Beck," sobbed the child,

throwing her arms around the woman's neck and crying as though her heart would break.

"Land sakes, what *is* the mattah?" she asked in alarm. She sat down on a mossy log, took off the white hat, and looked into the flushed, tearful face.

"Oh, it makes me so lonesome when you sing that way," wailed the Little Colonel. "I just can't 'tand it! Mom Beck, is my mothah's heart all broken? Is that why she is sick so much, and will it kill her suah 'nuff?"

"Who's been tellin' you such nonsense?" asked the woman sharply.

"Some ladies at the hotel were talkin' about it. They said that gran'fathah didn't love her any moah, an' it was just a-killin' her." Mom Beck frowned fiercely.

The child's grief was so deep and intense that she did not know just how to quiet her. Then she said decidedly, "Well, if that's all that's a-troublin' you, you can jus' get down an' walk home on yo' own laigs. Yo' mamma's a-grievin' cause yo' papa has to be away all the time. She's all wo'n out, too, with the work of movin', when she's nevah been use to doin' anything. But her heart isn't broke any moah'n my neck is."

The positive words and the decided toss

Mom Beck gave her head settled the matter for the Little Colonel. She wiped her eyes and stood up much relieved.

"Don't you nevah go to worryin' 'bout what you heahs," continued the woman. "I tell you p'intedly you cyarnt nevah b'lieve what you heahs."

"Why doesn't gran'fathah love my mothah?" asked the child as they came in sight of the cottage. She had puzzled over the knotty problem all the way home. "How can papas not love their little girls?"

"'Cause he's stubbo'n," was the unsatisfactory answer. "All the Lloyds is. Yo' mamma's stubbo'n, an' you's stubbo'n —"

"I'm not!" shrieked the Little Colonel, stamping her foot. "You sha'n't call me names!"

Then she saw a familiar white hand waving to her from the hammock, and she broke away from Mom Beck with very red cheeks and very bright eyes.

Cuddled close in her mother's arms, she had a queer feeling that she had grown a great deal older in that short afternoon.

Maybe she had. For the first time in her little life she kept her troubles to herself, and did not once mention the thought that was uppermost in her mind.

"Yo' great-aunt Sally Tylah is comin' this mawin'," said Mom Beck the day after their visit to the hotel. "Do fo' goodness' sake keep yo'self clean. I'se got too many spring chickens to dress to think 'bout dressin' you up again."

"Did I evah see her befo'?" questioned the Little Colonel.

"Why yes, the day we moved heah. Don't you know she came and stayed so long, and the rockah broke off the little white rockin'-chair when she sat down in it?"

"Oh, now I know!" laughed the child. "She's the big fat one with curls hangin' round her yeahs like shavin's. I don't like her, Mom Beck. She keeps a-kissin' me all the time, an' a-'queezin' me, an' tellin' me to sit on her lap an' be a little lady. Mom Beck, I *de'pise* to be a little lady."

There was no answer to her last remark. Mom Beck had stepped into the pantry for more eggs for the cake she was making.

"Fritz," said the Little Colonel, "yo' great-aunt Sally Tylah's comin' this mawnin', an' if you don't want to say 'howdy' to her you'll have to come with me."

A few minutes later a resolute little figure squeezed between the palings of the garden fence down by the gooseberry bushes.

"Now walk on your tiptoes, Fritz!" commanded the Little Colonel, "else somebody will call us back."

Mom Beck, busy with her extra baking, supposed she was with her mother on the shady vine-covered porch.

She would not have been singing quite so gayly if she could have seen half a mile up the road.

The Little Colonel was sitting in the weeds by the railroad track, deliberately taking off her shoes and stockings.

"Just like a little niggah," she said delightedly as she stretched out her bare feet. "Mom Beck says I ought to know bettah. But it does feel so good!"

No telling how long she might have sat there enjoying the forbidden pleasure of dragging her rosy toes through the warm dust, if she had not heard a horse's hoof-beats coming rapidly along.

"Fritz, its gran'fathah," she whispered in alarm, recognizing the erect figure of the rider in its spotless suit of white duck.

"Sh! lie down in the weeds, quick! Lie down, I say!"

They both made themselves as flat as possible, and lay there panting with the exertion of keeping still.

Presently the Little Colonel raised her head cautiously.

"Oh, he's gone down that lane!" she exclaimed. "Now you can get up." After a moment's deliberation she asked, "Fritz, would you rathah have some 'trawberries an' be tied up fo' runnin' away, or not be tied up and not have any of those nice tas'en 'trawberries?"

CHAPTER III.

Two hours later, Colonel Lloyd, riding down the avenue under the locusts, was surprised by a novel sight on his stately front steps.

Three little darkies and a big flop-eared hound were crouched on the bottom step, looking up at the Little Colonel, who sat just above them.

She was industriously stirring something in an old rusty pan with a big battered spoon.

"Now, May Lilly," she ordered, speaking to the largest and blackest of the group, "you run an' find some nice 'mooth pebbles to put in for raisins. Henry Clay, you go get me some moah sand. This is 'most too wet."

"Here, you little pickaninnies!" roared the Colonel as he recognized the cook's children. "What did I tell you about playing around here, tracking dirt all over my premises? You just chase back to the cabin where you belong!"

The sudden call startled Lloyd so that she dropped the pan, and the great mud pie turned upside down on the white steps.

"Well, you're a pretty sight!" said the Colonel as he glanced with disgust from her soiled dress and muddy hands to her bare feet.

He had been in a bad humor all morning. The sight of the steps covered with sand and muddy tracks gave him an excuse to give vent to his cross feelings.

It was one of his theories that a little girl should always be kept as fresh and dainty as a flower. He had never seen his own little daughter in such a plight as this, and she had never been allowed to step outside of her own room without her shoes and stockings.

"What does your mother mean," he cried savagely, "by letting you run barefooted around the country just like poor white trash? An' what are you playing with low-flung niggers for? Haven't you ever been taught any better? I suppose it's some of your father's miserable Yankee notions."

May Lilly, peeping around the corner of the house, rolled her frightened eyes from one angry face to the other. The same temper that glared from the face of the man, sitting erect in his saddle, seemed to be burning in the eyes of the child who stood so defiantly before him.

The same kind of scowl drew their eyebrows together darkly.

"Don't you talk that way to me," cried the

Little Colonel, trembling with a wrath she did not know how to express.

Suddenly she stooped, and snatching both hands full of mud from the overturned pie, flung it wildly over the spotless white coat.

Colonel Lloyd gasped with astonishment. It was the first time in his life he had ever been openly defied. The next moment his anger gave way to amusement.

"By George!" he chuckled admiringly. "The little thing has got spirit, sure enough. She's a Lloyd through and through. So that's why they call her the 'Little Colonel,' is it?"

There was a tinge of pride in the look he gave her haughty little head and flashing eyes.

"There, there, child!" he said soothingly. "I didn't mean to make you mad, when you were good enough to come and see me. It isn't often I have a little lady like you to pay me a visit."

"I didn't come to see you, suh," she answered indignantly as she started toward the gate. "I came to see May Lilly. But I nevah would have come inside yo' gate if I'd known you was goin' to hollah at me an' be so cross."

She was walking off with the air of an offended queen, when the Colonel remembered that if he allowed her to go away in that mood she would probably never set foot on his grounds again. Her display of temper had interested him immensely.

Now that he had laughed off his ill humor, he was anxious to see what other traits of character she possessed.

He wheeled his horse across the walk to bar her way, and quickly dismounted.

"Oh, now, wait a minute," he said in a coaxing tone. "Don't you want a nice big saucer of strawberries and cream before you go? Walker's picking some now. And you haven't seen my hothouse. It's just full of the loveliest flowers you ever saw. You like roses, don't you, and pinks and lilies and pansies?"

He saw he had struck the right chord as soon as he mentioned the flowers. The sullen look vanished as if by magic. Her face changed as suddenly as an April day.

"Oh, yes!" she cried, with a beaming smile. "I loves 'm bettah than anything!"

He tied his horse, and led the way to the conservatory. He opened the door for her to pass through, and then watched her closely to see what impression it would make on her. He had expected a delighted exclamation of surprise, for he had good reason to be proud of his rare plants. They were arranged with a true artist's eye for color and effect.

She did not say a word for a moment, but drew a long breath, while the delicate pink in her cheeks deepened and her eyes lighted up. Then she began going slowly from flower to flower, laying her face against the cool velvety purple of the pansies, touching the roses with her lips, and tilting the white lily-cups to look into their golden depths.

As she passed from one to another as lightly as a butterfly might have done, she began chanting in a happy undertone.

Ever since she had learned to talk she had a quaint little way of singing to herself. All the names that pleased her fancy she strung together in a crooning melody of her own.

There was no special tune. It sounded happy, although nearly always in a minor key.

"Oh, the jonquils an' the lilies!" she sang. "All white an' gold an' yellow. Oh, they're all a-smilin' at me, an' a-sayin' howdy! howdy!"

She was so absorbed in her intense enjoyment that she forgot all about the old Colonel. She was wholly unconscious that he was watching or listening.

"She really does love them," he thought complacently. "To see her face one would think she had found a fortune."

It was another bond between them.

After a while he took a small basket from the wall and began to fill it with his choicest blooms.

"You shall have these to take home," he said. "Now come into the house and get your strawberries."

She followed him reluctantly, turning back several times for one more long sniff of the delicious fragrance.

She was not at all like the Colonel's ideal of what a little girl should be, as she sat in one of the high, stiff chairs, enjoying her strawberries. Her dusty little toes wriggled around in the curls on Fritz's back, as she used him for a foot-stool. Her dress was draggled and dirty, and she kept leaning over to give the dog berries and cream from the spoon she was eating with herself.

He forgot all this, however, when she began to talk to him.

"My great-aunt Sally Tylah is to ou' house this mawnin'," she announced confidentially. "That's why we came off. Do you know my Aunt Sally Tylah?"

"Well, slightly!" chuckled the Colonel. "She was my wife's half sister. So you don't like her, eh? Well, I don't like her either."

He threw back his head and laughed heartily. The more the child talked the more entertaining he found her. He did not remember when he had ever been so amused before as he was by this tiny counterpart of himself.

When the last berry had vanished, she slipped down from the tall chair.

"Do you 'pose it's very late?" she asked in an anxious voice. "Mom Beck will be comin' for me soon."

"Yes, it is nearly noon," he answered. "It didn't do much good to run away from your Aunt Tyler; she'll see you after all."

"Well, she can't 'queeze me an' kiss me, 'cause I've been naughty, an I'll be put to bed like I was the othah day, just as soon as I get home. I 'most wish I was there now," she sighed. "It's so fa' an' the sun's so hot. I lost my sunbonnet when I was comin' heah, too."

Something in the tired, dirty face prompted the old Colonel to say, "Well, my horse hasn't been put away yet. I'll take you home on Maggie Boy."

The next moment he repented making such an offer, thinking what the neighbors might say if they should meet him on the road with Elizabeth's child in his arm.

But it was too late. He could not unclasp the trusting little hand that was slipped in his. He could not cloud the happiness of the eager little face by retracting his promise.

He swung himself into the saddle, with her in front.

Then he put his one arm around her with a firm clasp, as he reached forward to take the bridle.

"You couldn't take Fritz on behin', could

you?" she asked anxiously. "He's mighty ti'ed too."

"No," said the Colonel with a laugh. "Maggie Boy might object and throw us all off."

Hugging her basket of flowers close in her arms, she leaned her head against him contentedly as they cantered down the avenue.

"Look!" whispered all the locusts, waving their hands to each other excitedly. "Look! The master has his own again. The dear old times are coming back to us."

"How the trees blow!" exclaimed the child, looking up at the green arch overhead. "See! They's all a-noddin' tc each othah."

"We'll have to get my shoes an' 'tockin's," she said presently, when they were nearly home. "They're in that fence cawnah behin' a log."

The Colonel obediently got down and handed them to her. As he mounted again he saw a carriage coming toward them. He recognized one of his nearest neighbors. Striking the astonished Maggie Boy with his spur, he turned her across the railroad track, down the steep embankment, and into an unfrequented lane.

"This road is just back of your garden," he said. "Can you get through the fence if I take you there?"

"That's the way we came out," was the answer. "See that hole where the palin's are off?"

Just as he was about to lift her down, she put one arm around his neck, and kissed him softly on the cheek.

"Good by, gran'fatha'," she said in her most winning way. "I've had a mighty nice time." Then she added in a lower tone, "Kuse me fo' throwin' mud on yo' coat."

He held her close a moment, thinking nothing had ever before been half so sweet as the way she called him grandfather.

From that moment his heart went out to her as it had to little Tom and Elizabeth. It made no difference if her mother had forfeited his love. It made no difference if Jack Sherman was her father, and that the two men heartily hated each other.

It was his own little grandchild he held in his arms.

She had sealed the relationship with a trusting kiss.

"Child," he said huskily, "you will come and see me again, won't you, no matter if they do tell you not to? You shall have all the flowers and berries you want, and you can ride Maggie Boy as often as you please."

She looked up into his face. It was very familiar to her. She had looked at his portrait often, unconsciously recognizing a kindred spirit that she longed to know.

Her ideas of grandfathers gained from stories and observation led her to class them with fairy god-mothers. She had always wished for one.

The day they moved to Lloydsborough, Locust had been pointed out to her as her grandfather's home. From that time on she slipped away with Fritz on every possible occasion to peer through the gate, hoping for a glimpse of him.

"Yes, I'll come suah!" she promised. "I likes you just lots, gran'fathah!"

He watched her scramble through the hole in the fence. Then he turned his horse's head slowly homeward.

A scrap of white lying on the grass attracted his attention as he neared the gate.

"It's the lost sunbonnet," he said with a smile. He carried it into the house and hung it on the hat-rack in the wide front hall.

"Ole marse is crosser'n two sticks," growled Walker to the cook at dinner. "There ain't no livin' with him. What do you s'pose is the mattah?"

CHAPTER IV.

MOM BECK was busy putting lunch on the table when the Little Colonel looked in at the kitchen door.

So she did not see a little tramp, carrying her shoes in one hand and a basket in the other, who paused there a moment. But when she took up the pan of beaten biscuit she was puzzled to find that several were missing.

"It beats my time," she said aloud. "The parrot couldn't have reached them, an' Lloyd an' the dog have been in the pa'lah all mawnin'. Somethin' has jus' natch'ly done sperrited 'em away."

Fritz was gravely licking his lips, and the Little Colonel had her mouth full, when they suddenly made their appearance on the front porch.

Aunt Sally Tyler gave a little shriek and stopped rocking.

"Why, Lloyd Sherman!" gasped her mother in dismay. "Where *have* you been? I thought you were with Becky all the time. I was sure I heard you singing out there a little while ago."

"I've been to see my gran'fathah," said the child, speaking very fast. "I made mud pies on his front 'teps, an' we both of us got mad, an' I throwed mud on him, an' he gave me some 'trawberries an' all these flowers, an' brought me home on Maggie Boy."

She stopped out of breath.

Mrs. Tyler and her niece exchanged astonished glances.

"But, baby, how could you disgrace mother so by going up there looking like a dirty little beggar?"

"He didn't care," replied Lloyd calmly. "He made me promise to come again, no mattah if you all did tell me not to."

Just then Becky announced that lunch was ready, and carried the child away to make her presentable.

To Lloyd's great surprise she was not put to bed, but was allowed to go to the table as soon as she was dressed. It was not long until she had told every detail of the morning's experience.

While she was taking her afternoon nap, the two ladies sat out on the porch, gravely discussing all she had told them.

"It doesn't seem right for me to allow her to go there," said Mrs. Sherman, "after the way papa has treated us. I can never forgive him for all the terrible things he has said about Jack, and I know Jack can never be friends with him on account of what he has said about me. He has been so harsh and unjust that I don't want my little Lloyd to have anything to do with him. I wouldn't for worlds have him think that I encouraged her going there."

"Well, yes, I know," answered her aunt slowly. "But there are some things to consider besides your pride, Elizabeth. There's the child herself, you know. Now that Jack has lost so much, and your prospects are so uncertain, you ought to think of her interests. It would be a pity for Locust to go to strangers when it has been in your family for so many generations. That's what it certainly will do unless something turns up to interfere. Old Judge Woodard told me himself that your father had made a will, leaving everything he owns to some medical institution. Imagine Locust being turned into a sanitarium or a training school for nurses!"

"Dear old place!" said Mrs. Sherman, with tears in her eyes. "No one ever had a happier childhood than I passed under these old locusts. Every tree seems like a friend. I would be glad for Lloyd to enjoy the place as I did."

"I'd let her go as much as she pleases, Elizabeth. She's so much like the old Colonel that they ought to understand each other and get along capitally. Who knows, it might end in you all making up some day."

Mrs. Sherman raised her head haughtily. "No, indeed, Aunt Sally. I can forgive and forget much, but you are greatly mistaken if you think I can go to such lengths as that. He closed his doors against me with a curse, for no reason on earth but that the man I loved was born north of the Mason and Dixon line. There never was a nobler man living than Jack, and papa would have seen it if he hadn't deliberately shut his eyes and refused to look at him. He was just prejudiced and stubborn."

Aunt Sally said nothing, but her thoughts took the shape of Mom Beck's declaration, "The Lloyds is all stubbo'n."

"I wouldn't go through his gate now if he got down on his knees and begged me," continued Elizabeth hotly.

"It's too bad," exclaimed her aunt; "he was always so perfectly devoted to 'little daughter' as he used to call you. I don't like him myself. We never could get along together at all, because he is so high strung and overbearing. But I know it would have made your poor mother mighty unhappy if she could have foreseen all this."

Elizabeth sat with the tears dropping down on her little white hands, as her aunt proceeded to work on her sympathies in every way she could think of.

Presently Lloyd came out all fresh and rosy from her long nap, and went to play in the shade of the great beech trees that guarded the cottage.

"I never saw a child with such an influence over animals," said her mother as Lloyd came around the house with the parrot perched on the broom she was carrying. "She'll walk right up to any strange dog and make friends with it, no matter how savage-looking it is. And there's Polly, so old and cross that she screams and scolds dreadfully if any of us go near her. But Lloyd dresses her up in doll's clothes, puts paper bonnets on her, and makes her just as uncomfortable as she pleases. Look! that is one of her favorite amusements.'

The Little Colonel squeezed the parrot into a tiny doll carriage, and began to trundle it back and forth as fast as she could run.

"Ha! ha!" screamed the bird. "Polly is a lady! Oh, Lordy! I'm so happy!"

"She caught that from the washerwoman," laughed Mrs. Sherman. "I should think the poor thing would be dizzy from whirling around so fast."

"Quit that, chillun; stop yo' fussin'," screamed Polly as Lloyd grabbed her up and began to pin a shawl around her neck. She clucked angrily, but never once attempted to snap at the dimpled fingers that squeezed her tight. Suddenly, as if her patience was completely exhausted, she uttered a disdainful "Oh pshaw!" and flew up into an old cedar tree.

"Mothah! Polly won't play with me any moah," shrieked the child, flying into a rage. She stamped and scowled and grew red in the face. Then she began beating the trunk of the tree with the old broom she had been carrying.

"Did you ever see anything so much like the old Colonel?" said Mrs. Tyler in astonishment. "I wonder if she acted that way this morning."

"I don't doubt it at all," answered Mrs. Sherman. "She'll be over it in just a moment. These little spells never last long."

Mrs. Sherman was right. In a few moments Lloyd came up the walk, singing.

"I wish you'd tell me a pink story," she said coaxingly as she leaned against her mother's knee.

"Not now, dear; don't you see that I am busy talking to Aunt Sally? Run and ask Mom Beck for one."

"What on earth does she mean by a pink story?" asked Mrs. Tyler.

"Oh, she is so fond of colors. She is always asking for a pink or a blue or a white story. She wants everything in the story tinged with whatever color she chooses, — dresses, parasols, flowers, sky, even the icing on the cakes and the paper on the walls."

"What an odd little thing she is!" exclaimed Mrs. Tyler. "Isn't she lots of company for you?"

She need not have asked that question if she could have seen them that evening, sitting together in the early twilight.

Lloyd was in her mother's lap, leaning her head against her shoulder as they rocked slowly back and forth on the dark porch.

There was an occasional rattle of wheels along the road, a twitter of sleepy birds, a distant croaking of frogs.

Mom Beck's voice floated in from the kitchen, where she was stepping briskly around.

"Oh, the clouds hang heavy, an' it's gwine to rain.
Fa'well, my dyin' friends,"

she sang.

Lloyd put her arms closer around her mother's neck.

"Let's talk about Papa Jack," she said. "What you 'pose he's doin' now, 'way out west."

Elizabeth, feeling like a tired, homesick child herself, held her close, and was comforted as she listened to the sweet little voice talking about the absent father.

The moon came up after a while, and streamed in through the vines of the porch. The hazel eyes slowly closed as Elizabeth began to hum an old-time negro lullaby.

"Wondah if she'll run away to-morrow," whispered Mom Beck as she came out to carry her in the house.

"Who'd evah think now, lookin' at her pretty, innocent face, that she could be so naughty? Bless her little soul!"

The kind old black face was laid lovingly a moment against the fair soft cheek of the Little Colonel. Then she lifted her in her strong arms, and carried her gently away to bed.

CHAPTER V.

SUMMER lingers long among the Kentucky hills. Each passing day seemed fairer than the last to the Little Colonel, who had never before known anything of country life.

Roses climbed up and almost hid the small white cottage. Red birds sang in the woodbine. Squirrels chattered in the beeches. She was out of doors all day long.

Sometimes she spent hours watching the ants carry away the sugar she sprinkled for them. Sometimes she caught flies for an old spider that had his den under the porch steps.

"He is an ogah" (ogre), she explained to Fritz. "He's bewitched me so's I have to kill whole families of flies for him to eat."

She was always busy and always happy.

Before June was half over it got to be a common occurrence for Walker to ride up to the gate on the Colonel's horse. The excuse was always to have a passing word with Mom Beck. But before he rode away, the Little Colonel was generally mounted in front of him. It was not long before she felt almost as much at home at Locust as she did at the cottage.

The neighbors began to comment on it after a while. "He will surely make up with Elizabeth at this rate," they said. But at the end of the summer the father and daughter had not even had a passing glimpse of each other.

One day, late in September, as the Little Colonel clattered up and down the hall with her grandfather's spur buckled on her tiny foot, she called back over her shoulder: "Papa Jack's comin' home to-morrow."

The Colonel paid no attention.

"I say," she repeated, "Papa Jack's comin' home to-morrow."

"Well," was the gruff response. "Why couldn't he stay where he was? I suppose you won't want to come here any more after he gets back."

"No, I 'pose not," she answered so carelessly that he was conscious of a very jealous feeling.

"Chilluns always like to stay with their fathahs when they's nice as my Papa Jack is."

The old man growled something behind his newspaper that she did not hear. He would have been glad to choke this man who had come between him and his only child, and he hated him worse than ever when he realized what a large place he held in Lloyd's little heart.

She did not go back to Locust the next day, nor for weeks after that.

She was up almost as soon as Mom Beck next morning, thoroughly enjoying the bustle of preparation.

She had a finger in everything, from polishing the silver to turning the ice-cream freezer.

Even Fritz was scrubbed till he came out of his bath with his curls all white and shining. He was proud of himself, from his silky bangs to the tip of his tasselled tail.

Just before train time, the Little Colonel

stuck his collar full of late pink roses, and stood back to admire the effect. Her mother came to the door, dressed for the evening. She wore an airy-looking dress of the palest, softest blue. There was a white rosebud caught in her dark hair. A bright color, as fresh as Lloyd's own, tinged her cheeks, and the glad light in her brown eyes made them unusually brilliant.

Lloyd jumped up and threw her arms about her. "Oh, mothah," she cried, "you an' Fritz is *so* bu'ful!"

The engine whistled up the road at the crossing. "Come, we have just time to get to the station," said Mrs. Sherman, holding out her hand.

They went through the gate, down the narrow path that ran beside the dusty road. The train had just stopped in front of the little station when they reached it.

A number of gentlemen, coming out from the city to spend Sunday at the hotel, came down the steps.

They glanced admiringly from the beautiful, girlish face of the mother to the happy child dancing impatiently up and down at her side. They could not help smiling at Fritz as he frisked about in his imposing rose-collar.

"Why, where's Papa Jack?" asked Lloyd in

distress as passenger after passenger stepped down. "Isn't he goin' to come?"

The tears were beginning to gather in her eyes, when she saw him in the door of the car; not hurrying along to meet them as he always used to come, so full of life and vigor, but leaning heavily on the porter's shoulder, looking very pale and weak.

Lloyd looked up at her mother, from whose face every particle of color had faded. Mrs. Sherman gave a low, frightened cry as she sprang forward to meet him.

"Oh, Jack! what is the matter? What has happened to you?" she exclaimed as he took her in his arms. The train had gone on, and they were left alone on the platform.

"Just a little sick spell," he answered with a smile. "We had a fire out at the mines, and I overtaxed myself some. I've had fever ever since, and it has pulled me down considerably."

"I must send somebody for a carriage," she said, looking around anxiously.

"No, indeed," he protested. "It's only a few steps; I can walk it as well as not. The sight of you and the baby has made me stronger already."

He sent a colored boy on ahead with his

valise, and they walked slowly up the path, with Fritz running wildly around them, barking a glad welcome.

"How sweet and homelike it all looks!" he said as he stepped into the hall, where Mom Beck was just lighting the lamps. Then he sank down on the couch, completely exhausted, and wearily closed his eyes.

The Little Colonel looked at his white face in alarm. All the gladness seemed to have been taken out of the homecoming.

Her mother was busy trying to make him comfortable, and paid no attention to the disconsolate little figure wandering about the house alone. Mom Beck had gone for the doctor.

The supper was drying up in the warming oven. The ice-cream was melting in the freezer. Nobody seemed to care. There was no one to notice the pretty table with its array of flowers and cut glass and silver.

When Mom Beck came back, Lloyd ate all by herself, and then sat out on the kitchen door-step while the doctor made his visit.

She was just going mournfully off to bed with an aching lump in her throat, when her mother opened the door.

"Come tell papa good night," she said. "He's lots better now."

She climbed up on the bed beside him, and buried her face on his shoulder to hide the tears she had been trying to keep back all evening.

"How the child has grown!" he exclaimed. "Do you notice, Beth, how much plainer she talks? She does not seem at all like the baby I left last spring. Well, she'll soon be six years old, — a real little woman. She'll be papa's little comfort."

The ache in her throat was all gone after that. She romped with Fritz all the time she was undressing.

Papa Jack was worse next morning. It was hard for Lloyd to keep quiet when the late September sunshine was so gloriously yellow and the whole outdoors seemed so wide awake.

She tiptoed out of the darkened room where her father lay, and swung on the front gate until she saw the doctor riding up on his bay horse. It seemed to her that the day never would pass.

Mom Beck, rustling around in her best dress ready for church, that afternoon, took pity on the lonesome child.

"Go get yo' best hat, honey," she said, "an' I'll take you with me."

It was one of the Little Colonel's greatest pleasures to be allowed to go to the colored church.

She loved to listen to the singing, and would sit perfectly motionless while the sweet voices blended like the chords of some mighty organ as they sent the old hymns rolling heavenward.

Service had already commenced by the time they took their seats. Nearly everybody in the congregation was swaying back and forth in time to the mournful melody of "Sinnah, sinnah, where's you boun'?"

One old woman across the aisle began clapping her hands together, and repeated in a sing-song tone, "Oh, Lordy! I'm so happy!"

"Why, that's just what our parrot says," exclaimed Lloyd, so much surprised that she spoke right out loud.

Mom Beck put her handkerchief over her mouth, and a general smile went around.

After that the child was very quiet until the time came to take the collection. She always enjoyed this part of the service more than anything else. Instead of passing baskets around, each person was invited to come forward and lay his offering on the table.

Woolly heads wagged and many feet kept time to the tune:

> "Oh! I'se boun' to git to glory.
> Hallelujah! Le' me go!"

The Little Colonel proudly marched up with

Mom Beck's contribution, and then watched the others pass down the aisle. One young girl in a gorgeously trimmed dress paraded up to the table several times, singing at the top of her voice.

"Look at that good-fo'-nothin' Lize Richa'ds," whispered Mom Beck's nearest neighbor, with a sniff. "She done got a nickel changed into pennies so she could ma'ch up an' show herself five times."

It was nearly sundown when they started home. A tall colored man, wearing a high silk hat and carrying a gold-headed cane, joined them on the way out.

"Howdy, Sistah Po'tah," he said, gravely shaking hands. "That was a fine disco'se we had the pleasuah of listenin' to this evenin'."

"'Deed it was, Brothah Fostah," she answered. "How's all up yo' way?"

The Little Colonel, running on after a couple of white butterflies, paid no attention to the conversation until she heard her own name mentioned.

"Mistah Sherman came home last night, I heah."

"Yes, but not to stay long, I'm afraid. He's a mighty sick man, if I'm any judge. He's down with fevah, — regulah typhoid. He doesn't look to me like he's long for this world. What's to become of poah Miss 'Lizabeth if that's the case, is moah'n *I* know."

"We mustn't cross the bridge till we come to it, Sistah Po'tah," he suggested.

"I know that; but a lookin'-glass broke yeste'day mawnin' when nobody had put fingah on it. An' his picture fell down off the wall while I was sweepin' the pa'lah. Pete said his dawg done howl all night last night, an' I've dremp three times hand runnin' 'bout muddy watah."

Mom Beck felt a little hand clutch her skirts, and turned to see a frightened little face looking anxiously up at her.

"Now what's the mattah with you, honey?" she asked. "I'm only a-tellin' Mistah Fostah about some silly old signs my mammy used to believe in. But they don't mean nothin' at all."

Lloyd couldn't have told why she was unhappy. She had not understood all that Mom

Beck had said, but her sensitive little mind was shadowed by a foreboding of trouble.

The shadow deepened as the days passed. Papa Jack got worse instead of better. There were times when he did not recognize any one, and talked wildly of things that had happened out at the mines.

All the long beautiful October went by, and still he lay in the darkened room. Lloyd wandered listlessly from place to place, trying to keep out of the way and to make as little trouble as possible.

"I'm a real little woman now," she repeated proudly whenever she was allowed to pound ice or carry fresh water. "I'm papa's little comfort."

One cold, frosty evening she was standing in the hall, when the doctor came out of the room and began to put on his overcoat.

Her mother followed him to take his directions for the night.

He was an old friend of the family's. Elizabeth had climbed on his knees many a time when she was a child. She loved this faithful, white-haired old doctor almost as dearly as she had her father.

"My daughter," he said kindly, laying his hand on her shoulder, "you are wearing yourself out, and will be down yourself if you are not careful. You must have a professional nurse. No telling how long this is going to last. As soon as Jack is able to travel you must have a change of climate."

Her lips trembled. "We can't afford it, doctor," she said. "Jack has been too sick from the very first to talk about business. He always said a woman should not be worried with such matters, anyway. I don't know what arrangements he has made out west. For all I know, the little I have in my purse now may be all that stands between us and the poorhouse."

The doctor drew on his gloves.

"Why don't you tell your father how matters are?" he asked.

Then he saw he had ventured a step too far.

"I believe Jack would rather die than take help from his hands," she answered, drawing herself up proudly. Her eyes flashed. "I would, too, as far as I am concerned myself."

Then a tender look came over her pale, tired face as she added gently, "But I'd do anything on earth to help Jack get well."

The doctor cleared his throat vigorously, and bolted out with a gruff good night. As he rode past Locust, he took solid satisfaction in shaking his fist at the light in an upper window.

CHAPTER VI.

THE Little Colonel followed her mother to the dining-room, but paused on the threshold as she saw her throw herself into Mom Beck's arms and burst out crying.

"Oh, Becky!" she sobbed, "what is going to become of us? The doctor says we must have a professional nurse, and we must go away from here soon. There are only a few dollars left in my purse, and I don't know what we'll do when they are gone. I just *know* Jack is going to die, and then I'll die too, and then what will become of the baby?"

Mom Beck sat down and took the trembling form in her arms.

"There, there!" she said soothingly, "have yo' cry out. It will do you good. Poah chile! all wo'n out with watchin' an' worry. Ne'm min', ole Becky is as good as a dozen nuhses yet. I'll get Judy to come up an' look aftah the kitchen. An' nobody ain' gwine to die, honey. Don't you go to slayin' all you's got befo' you's called on to do it. The good Lawd is goin' to pahvide fo' us same as Abraham."

The last Sabbath's sermon was still fresh in her mind.

"If we only hold out faithful, there's boun' to be a ram caught by the hawns some place, even if we haven't got eyes to see through the thickets. The Lawd will pahvide whethah it's a burnt offerin' or a meal's vittles. He sho'ly will."

Lloyd crept away frightened. It seemed such an awful thing to her to see her mother cry.

All at once her bright, happy world had changed to such a strange, uncertain place. She felt as if all sorts of terrible things were about to happen.

She went into the parlor and crawled into a dark corner under the piano, feeling that there was no place to go for comfort, since the one who had always kissed away her little troubles was so heartbroken herself.

There was a patter of soft feet across the carpet, and Fritz poked his sympathetic nose into her face. She put her arms around him and laid her head against his curly back with a desolate sob.

It is pitiful to think how much imaginative children suffer through their wrong conception of things.

She had seen the little roll of bills in her mother's pocketbook. She had seen how much smaller it grew every time it was taken out to pay for the expensive wines and medicines that had to be bought so often. She had heard her mother tell the doctor that was all that stood between them and the poorhouse.

There was no word known to the Little Colonel that brought such thoughts of horror as the word poorhouse.

Her most vivid recollection of her life in New York was something that happened a few weeks before they left there. One day in the park she ran away from the maid, who, instead of Mom Beck, had taken charge of her that afternoon.

When the angry woman found her, she frightened her almost into a spasm by telling her what always happened to naughty children who ran away.

"They take all their pretty clothes off," she said, "and dress them up in old things made of bed ticking. Then they take'm to the poorhouse, where nobody but beggars live. They don't have anything to eat but cabbage and corn-dodger, and they have to eat that out of tin pans. And they just have a pile of straw to sleep in."

On their way home she had pointed out to the frightened child a poor woman who was grubbing in an ash barrel.

"That's the way people get to look who live in poorhouses," she said.

It was this memory that was troubling the Little Colonel now.

"Oh, Fritz!" she whispered, with the tears running down her cheeks, "I can't beah to think of my pretty mothah goin' there. That woman's eyes were all red, an' her hair was jus' awful. She was so bony an' stahved-lookin'. It would jus' kill poah Papa Jack to lie on straw an' eat out of a tin pan. I *know* it would!"

When Mom Beck opened the door, hunting her, the room was so dark that she would have gone away if the dog had not come running out from under the piano.

"You heah too, chile?" she asked in surprise. "I have to go down now an' see if I can get Judy to come help to-morrow. Do you think you can undress yo'self to-night?"

"Of co'se," answered the Little Colonel. Mom Beck was in such a hurry to be off that she did not notice the tremble in the voice that answered her.

"Well, the can'le is lit in yo' room. So run along now like a nice little lady, an' don't bothah yo' mamma. She got her hands full already."

"All right," answered the child.

A quarter of an hour later she stood in her little white nightgown with her hand on the door knob.

She opened the door just a crack and peeped in. Her mother laid her finger on her lips and beckoned silently. In another instant Lloyd was in her lap. She had cried herself quiet in the dark corner under the piano; but there was something more pathetic in her eyes than tea: It was the expression of one who understood and sympathized.

"Oh, mothah," she whispered, "we does have such lots of troubles."

"Yes, chickabiddy, but I hope they will soon be over now," was the answer as the anxious face tried to smile bravely for the child's sake. "Papa is sleeping so nicely now he is sure to be better in the morning."

That comforted the Little Colonel some, but for days she was haunted by the fear of the poorhouse.

Every time her mother paid out any money she looked anxiously to see how much was still left. She wandered about the place, touching the trees and vines with caressing hands, feeling that she might soon have to leave them.

She loved them all so dearly, — every stick

and stone, and even the stubby old snowball bushes that never bloomed.

Her dresses were outgrown and faded, but no one had any time or thought to spend on getting her new ones. A little hole began to come in the toe of each shoe.

She was still wearing her summer sunbonnet, although the days were getting frosty.

She was a proud little thing. It mortified her for any one to see her looking so shabby. Still she uttered no word of complaint for fear of lessening the little amount in the pocketbook, that her mother had said stood between them and the poorhouse.

She sat with her feet tucked under her when any one called.

"I wouldn't mind bein' a little beggah so much myself," she thought, "but I jus' can't have my bu'ful sweet mothah lookin' like that awful red-eyed woman."

One day the doctor called Mrs. Sherman out into the hall. "I have just come from your father's," he said. "He is suffering from a severe attack of rheumatism. He is confined to his room, and is positively starving for company. He told me he would give anything in the world to have his little grandchild with him. There were tears in his eyes when he said it, and that means a good deal from him. He fairly idolizes her. The servants have told him she mopes around and is getting thin and pale. He is afraid she will come down with the fever too. He told me to use any stratagem I liked to get her there. But I think it's better to tell you frankly how matters stand. It will do the child good to have a change, Elizabeth, and I solemnly think you ought to let her go, for a week at least."

"But, doctor, she has never been away from me a single night in her life. She'd die of home sickness, and I know she'll never consent to leave me. Then suppose Jack should get worse — "

"We'll suppose nothing of the kind," he interrupted brusquely. "Tell Becky to pack up her things. Leave Lloyd to me. I'll get her consent without any trouble."

"Come, Colonel," he called as he left the house. "I'm going to take you a little ride."

No one ever knew what the kind old fellow said to her to induce her to go to her grandfather's.

She came back from her ride looking brighter than she had in a long time. She felt that in some way, although in what way she could not understand, her going would help them to escape the dreaded poorhouse.

"Don't send Mom Beck with me," she pleaded, when the time came to start. "You come with me, mothah."

Mrs. Sherman had not been past the gate for weeks, but she could not refuse the coaxing hands that clung to hers.

It was a dull, dreary day. There was a chilling hint of snow in the damp air. The leaves whirled past them with a mournful rustling.

Mrs. Sherman turned up the collar of Lloyd's cloak.

"You must have a new one soon," she said with a sigh. "Maybe one of mine could be made over for you. And those poor little shoes! I must think to send to town for a new pair."

The walk was over so soon. The Little Colonel's heart beat fast as they came in sight of the gate. She winked bravely to keep back the tears; for she had promised the doctor not to let her mother see her cry.

A week seemed such a long time to look forward to.

She clung to her mother's neck, feeling that she could never give her up so long.

"Tell me good-by, baby dear," said Mrs. Sherman, feeling that she could not trust herself to stay much longer. "It is too cold for you to stand here. Run on, and I'll watch you till you get inside the door."

The Little Colonel started bravely down the avenue, with Fritz at her heels. Every few

steps she turned to look back and kiss her hand.

Mrs. Sherman watched her through a blur of tears. It had been nearly seven years since she had last stood at that old gate. Such a crowd of memories came rushing up!

She looked again. There was a flutter of a white handkerchief as the Little Colonel and Fritz went up the steps. Then the great front door closed behind them

CHAPTER VII.

THAT early twilight hour just before the lamps were lit was the lonesomest one the Little Colonel had ever spent.

Her grandfather was asleep upstairs. There was a cheery wood fire crackling on the hearth of the big fireplace in the hall, but the great house was so still. The corners were full of shadows.

She opened the front door with a wild longing to run away.

"Come, Fritz," she said, closing the door softly behind her, "let's go down to the gate."

The air was cold. She shivered as they raced along under the bare branches of the locusts. She leaned against the gate, peering out through the bars. The road stretched white through the gathering darkness, in the direction of the little cottage.

"Oh, I want to go home so bad!" she sobbed. "I want to see my mothah."

She laid her hand irresolutely on the latch, pushed the gate ajar, and then hesitated.

"No, I promised the doctah I'd stay," she thought. "He said I could help mothah and

Papa Jack, both of 'em, by stayin' heah, an' I'll do it."

Fritz, who had pushed himself through the partly opened gate to rustle around among the dead leaves outside, came bounding back with something in his mouth.

"Heah, suh!" she called. "Give it to me!" He dropped a small gray kid glove in her outstretched hand. "Oh, it's mothah's!" she cried. "I reckon she dropped it when she was tellin' me good-by. Oh you deah old dog fo' findin' it."

She laid the glove against her cheek as fondly as if it had been her mother's soft hand. There was something wonderfully comforting in the touch.

As they walked slowly back toward the house she rolled it up and put it lovingly away in her tiny apron pocket.

All that week it was a talisman whose touch helped the homesick little soul to be brave and womanly.

When Maria, the colored housekeeper, went into the hall to light the lamps, the Little Colonel was sitting on the big fur rug in front of the fire, talking contentedly to Fritz, who lay with his curly head in her lap.

"You all's goin' to have tea in the Cun'l's

room to-night," said Maria. "He tole me to tote it up soon as he rung the bell."

"There it goes now," cried the child, jumping up from the rug.

She followed Maria up the wide stairs. The Colonel was sitting in a large easy-chair, wrapped in a gayly flowered dressing-gown, that made his hair look unusually white by contrast. His dark eyes were intently watching the door. As it opened to let the Little Colonel pass through, a very tender smile lighted up his stern face.

"So you did come to see grandpa after all," he cried triumphantly. "Come here and give me a kiss. Seems to me you've been staying away a mighty long time."

As she stood beside him with his arm around her, Walker came in with a tray full of dishes.

"We're going to have a regular little tea-party," said the Colonel.

Lloyd watched with sparkling eyes as Walker set out the rare old-fashioned dishes. There was a fat little silver sugar-bowl with a butterfly perched on each side to form the handles, and there was a slim, graceful cream-pitcher shaped like a lily.

"They belonged to your great-great-grandmother," said the Colonel, "and they're going to be yours some day if you grow up and have a house of your own."

The expression on her beaming face was worth a fortune to the Colonel.

When Walker pushed her chair up to the table, she turned to her grandfather with shining eyes.

"Oh, it's just like a pink story," she cried, clapping her hands. "The shades on the can'les, the icin' on the cake, an' the posies in the bowl, — why, even the jelly is that colah too. Oh, my darlin' little teacup! It's jus' like a pink rosebud! I'm *so* glad I came!"

The Colonel smiled at the success of his plan. In the depths of his satisfaction he even had a plate of quail and toast set down on the hearth for Fritz.

"This is the nicest pahty I evah was at," remarked the Little Colonel as Walker helped her to jam the third time.

Her grandfather chuckled.

"Blackberry jam always makes me think of Tom," he said. "Did you ever hear what your uncle Tom did when he was a little fellow in dresses?"

She shook her head gravely.

"Well, the children were all playing hide-and-seek one day. They hunted high and they hunted low after everybody else had been caught, but they couldn't find Tom. At last they began to call, 'Home free! You can come home free!' but he did not come. When he had been hidden so long they were frightened about him they went to their mother and told her he wasn't to be found anywhere. She looked down the well and behind the fire-boards in the fireplaces. They called and called till they were out of breath. Finally she thought of looking in the big dark pantry where she kept her fruit. There stood Mister Tom. He had opened a jar of blackberry jam, and was just going for it with both hands. The jam was all over his face and hair and little gingham apron, and even up his wrists. He was the funniest sight I ever saw."

The Little Colonel laughed heartily at his description, and begged for more stories. Before he knew it he was back in the past with his little Tom and Elizabeth.

Nothing could have entertained the child more than these scenes he recalled of her mother's childhood.

"All her old playthings are up in the garret," he said as they rose from the table. "I'll have them brought down to-morrow. There's a doll I brought her from New Orleans once when she was about your size. No telling what it looks like now, but it was a beauty when it was new."

Lloyd clapped her hands and spun around the room like a top.

"Oh, I'm so glad I came!" she exclaimed for the third time. "What did she call the doll, gran'fathah, do you remembah?"

"I never paid much attention to such things," he answered, "but I do remember the name of this one, because she named it for her mother, — Amanthis."

"Amanthis," repeated the child dreamily as she leaned against his knee. "I think that is a lovely name, gran'fathah. I wish they had called me that." She repeated it softly several times. "It sounds like the wind a-blowin' through white clovah, doesn't it?"

"It is a beautiful name to me, my child," answered the old man, laying his hand tenderly on her soft hair, "but not so beautiful as the woman who bore it. She was the fairest flower of all Kentucky. There never was another lived as sweet and gentle as your grandmother Amanthis."

He stroked her hair absently and gazed into the fire. He scarcely noticed when she slipped away from him.

She buried her face a moment in the bowl of pink roses. Then she went to the window and drew back the curtain. Leaning her head against the window-sill, she began stringing on the thread of a tune the things that just then thrilled her with a sense of their beauty.

"Oh, the locus' trees a-blowin'," she sang softly. "An' the moon a-shinin' through them. An' the starlight an' pink roses; an' Amanthis — an' Amanthis!"

She hummed it over and over until Walker had finished carrying the dishes away.

It was a strange thing that the Colonel's unfrequent moods of tenderness were like those warm days that they call weather breeders.

They were sure to be followed by a change of atmosphere. This time as the fierce rheumatic pain came back he stormed at Walker and scolded him for everything he did and everything he left undone.

When Maria came up to put Lloyd to bed, Fritz was tearing around the room barking at his shadow.

"Put that dog out M'ria!" roared the Colonel, almost crazy with its antics. "Take it downstairs and put it out of the house, I say! Nobody but a heathen would let a dog sleep in the house, anyway."

The homesick feeling began to creep over Lloyd again. She had expected to keep Fritz in her room at night for company. But for the touch of the little glove in her pocket, she would have said something ugly to her grandfather when he spoke so harshly.

His own ill-humor was reflected in her scowl as she followed Maria down the stairs to drive Fritz out into the dark.

They stood a moment in the open door, after Maria had slapped him with her apron to make him go off the porch.

"Oh, look at the new moon!" cried Lloyd,

pointing to the slender crescent in the autumn sky.

"I'se feared to, honey," answered Maria, "less I should see it through the trees. That 'ud bring me bad luck for a month, suah. I'll go out on the lawn where it's open, an' look at it ovah my right shouldah."

While they were walking backward down the path, intent on reaching a place where they could have an uninterrupted view of the moon, Fritz sneaked around to the other end of the porch.

No one was watching. He slipped into the house as noiselessly as his four soft feet could carry him.

Maria, going through the dark upper hall with a candle held high above her head and Lloyd clinging to her skirts, did not see a tasselled tail swinging along in front of her. It disappeared under the big bed when she led Lloyd into the room next the old Colonel's.

The child felt very sober while she was being put to bed.

The furniture was heavy and dark. An ugly portrait of a cross old man in a wig frowned at her from over the mantel. The dancing fire-light made his eyes frightfully life-like.

The bed was so high she had to climb on a

chair to get in. She heard Maria's heavy feet go shuffling down the stairs. A door banged. Then it was so still she could hear the clock tick in the next room.

It was the first time in all her life that her mother had not come to kiss her good night.

Her lips quivered, and a big tear rolled down on the pillow.

She reached out to the chair beside her bed, where her clothes were hanging, and felt in her apron pocket for the little glove. She sat up in bed, and looked at it in the dim firelight. Then she held it against her face. "Oh, I want my mothah! I want my mothah!" she sobbed in a heartbroken whisper.

Laying her head on her knees, she began to cry quietly, but with great sobs that nearly choked her.

There was a rustling under the bed. She lifted her wet face in alarm. Then she smiled through her tears, for there was Fritz, her own dear dog, and not an unknown horror waiting to grab her.

He stood on his hind legs, eagerly trying to lap away her tears with his friendly red tongue.

She clasped him in her arms with an ecstatic hug. "Oh, you're such a comfort!" she whispered. "I can go to sleep now."

She spread her apron on the bed, and motioned him to jump. With one spring he was beside her.

It was nearly midnight, when the door from the Colonel's room was noiselessly opened.

The old man stirred the fire gently until it burst into a bright flame. Then he turned to the bed. "You rascal!" he whispered, looking at Fritz, who raised his head quickly with a threatening look in his wicked eyes.

Lloyd lay with one hand stretched out, holding the dog's protecting paw. The other held something against her tear-stained cheek.

"What under the sun!" he thought as he drew it gently from her fingers. The little glove lay across his hand, slim and aristocratic-looking. He knew instinctively whose it was. "Poor little thing's been crying," he thought. "She wants Elizabeth. And so do I! And so do I!" his heart cried out with bitter longing. "It's never been like home since she left."

He laid the glove back on her pillow, and went to his room.

"If Jack Sherman should die," he said to himself many times that night, "then she would come home again. Oh, little daughter, little daughter! why did you ever leave me?"

CHAPTER VIII.

THE first thing that greeted the Little Colonel's eyes when she opened them next morning was her mother's old doll. Maria had laid it on the pillow beside her.

It was beautifully dressed, although in a queer, old-fashioned style that seemed very strange to the child.

She took it up with careful fingers, remembering its great age. Maria had warned her not to waken her grandfather, so she admired it in whispers.

"Jus' think, Fritz," she exclaimed, "this doll has seen my gran'mothah Amanthis, an' it's named for her. My mothah wasn't any bigger'n me when she played with it. I think it is the loveliest doll I evah saw in my whole life."

Fritz gave a jealous bark.

"Sh!" commanded his little mistress. "Didn't you heah M'ria say, 'Fo' de Lawd's sake don't wake up ole Marse?' Why don't you mind?"

The Colonel was not in the best of humors after such a wakeful night, but the sight of her happiness made him smile in spite of himself, when she danced into his room with the doll.

She had eaten an early breakfast and gone back upstairs to examine the other toys that were spread out in her room.

The door between the two rooms was ajar. All the time he was dressing and taking his coffee he could hear her talking to some one. He supposed it was Maria. But as he glanced over his mail he heard the Little Colonel saying, "May Lilly, do you know about Billy Goat Gruff? Do you want me to tell you that story?"

He leaned forward until he could look through the narrow opening of the door. Two heads were all he could see, — Lloyd's, soft-haired and golden, May Lilly's, covered with dozens of tightly braided little black tails.

He was about to order May Lilly back to the cabin, when he remembered the scene that followed the last time he had done so. He concluded to keep quiet and listen.

"Billy Goat Gruff was so fat," the story went on, "jus' as fat as gran'fathah."

The Colonel glanced up with an amused smile at the fine figure reflected in an opposite mirror.

"Trip-trap, trip-trap, went Billy Goat Gruff's little feet ovah the bridge to the giant's house."

Just at this point Walker, who was putting

things in order, closed the door between the rooms.

"Open that door, you black rascal!" called the Colonel, furious at the interruption.

In his haste to obey, Walker knocked over a pitcher of water that had been left on the floor beside the washstand.

Then the Colonel yelled at him to be quick about mopping it up, so that by the time the door was finally opened, Lloyd was finishing her story.

The Colonel looked in just in time to see her put her hands to her temples, with her fore-fingers protruding from her forehead like horns. She said in a deep voice, as she brandished them at May Lilly, "With my two long speahs I'll poke yo' eyeballs through yo' yeahs."

The little darky fell back giggling. "That sut'n'y was like a billy-goat. We had one once that 'ud make a body step around mighty peart. It slip up behine me one mawnin' on the poach, an' fo' a while I thought my haid was buss open suah. I got up toreckly, though, an' I cotch him, and when I done got through, mistah Billy-goat feel po'ly moah'n a week. He sut'n'y did."

Walker grinned, for he had witnessed the scene.

Just then Maria put her head in at the door to say, "May Lilly, yo' mammy's callin' you."

Lloyd and Fritz followed her noisily down stairs. Then for nearly an hour it was very quiet in the great house.

The Colonel, looking out of the window, could see Lloyd playing hide-and-seek with Fritz under the bare locust trees.

When she came in her cheeks were glowing from her run in the frosty air. Her eyes shone like stars, and her face was radiant.

"See what I've found down in the dead leaves," she cried. "A little blue violet, bloomin' all by itself."

She brought a tiny cup from the next room, that belonged to the set of doll dishes, and put the violet in it.

"There!" she said, setting it on the table at her grandfather's elbow. "Now I'll put Amanthis in this chair, where you can look at her, an' you won't get lonesome while I'm playin' outdoors."

He drew her toward him and kissed her.

"Why, how cold your hands are!" he exclaimed. "Staying in this warm room all the time makes me forget it is so wintry outdoors. I don't believe you are dressed warmly enough. You ought not to wear sunbonnets this time of year."

Then for the first time he noticed her outgrown cloak and shabby shoes.

"What are you wearing these old clothes for?" he said impatiently. "Why didn't they dress you up when you were going visiting? It isn't showing proper respect to send you off in the oldest things you've got."

It was a sore point with the Little Colonel. It hurt her pride enough to have to wear old clothes without being scolded for it. Besides, she felt that in some way her mother was being blamed for what could not be helped.

"They's the best I've got," she answered, proudly choking back the tears. " don't need any new ones, 'cause maybe we'll be goin' away pretty soon."

"Going away!" he echoed blankly. "Where?"

She did not answer until he repeated the question. Then she turned her back on him, and started toward the door. The tears she was too proud to let him see were running down her face.

"We's goin' to the poah-house," she exclaimed defiantly, "jus' as soon as the money in the pocketbook is used up. It was nearly gone when I came away."

Here she began to sob, as she fumbled at the door she could not see to open.

"I'm goin' home to my mothah right now. She loves me if my clothes are old and ugly."

"Why, Lloyd," called the Colonel, amazed and distressed by her sudden burst of grief. "Come here to grandpa. Why didn't you tell me so before?"

The face, the tone, the outstretched arm, all drew her irresistibly to him. It was a relief to lay her head on his shoulder and unburden herself of the fear that had haunted her so many days.

With her arms around his neck, and the precious little head held close to his heart, the old Colonel was in such a softened mood that he would have promised anything to comfort her.

"There, there," he said soothingly, stroking her hair with a gentle hand, when she had told him all her troubles. "Don't you worry about that, my dear. Nobody is going to eat out of tin pans and sleep on straw. Grandpa just won't let them."

She sat up and wiped her eyes on her apron. "But Papa Jack would *die* befo' he'd take help from you," she wailed. "An' so would mothah. I heard her tell the doctah so."

The tender expression on the Colonel's face changed to one like flint, but he kept on stroking her hair.

"People sometimes change their minds," he said grimly. "I wouldn't worry over a little thing like that if I were you. Don't you want to run downstairs and tell M'ria to give you a piece of cake?"

"Oh, yes," she exclaimed, smiling up at him. "I'll bring you some too."

When the first train went into Louisville that afternoon, Walker was on board with an order in his pocket to one of the largest dry goods establishments in the city. When he came out again that evening, he carried a large box into the Colonel's room.

Lloyd's eyes shone as she looked into it. There was an elegant fur-trimmed cloak, a pair of dainty shoes, and a muff that she caught up with a shriek of delight.

"What kind of a thing is this?" grumbled the Colonel as he took out a hat that had been carefully packed in one corner of the box. "I told them to send the most stylish thing they had. It looks like a scare-crow," he continued, as he set it askew on the child's head.

She snatched it off to look at it herself. "Oh, it's jus' like Emma Louise Wyfo'd's!" she exclaimed. "You didn't put it on straight. See! This is the way it goes."

She climbed up in front of the mirror, and put it on as she had seen Emma Louise wear hers.

"Well, it's a regular Napoleon hat," exclaimed the Colonel, much pleased. "So little girls nowadays have taken to wearing soldier's caps, have they? It's right becoming to you with your short hair. Grandpa is real proud of his 'little Colonel.'"

She gave him the military salute he had taught her, and then ran to throw her arms around him. "Oh, gran'fathah!" she exclaimed between her kisses, "you'se jus' as good as Santa Claus, every bit."

The Colonel's rheumatism was better next day; so much better that toward evening he walked downstairs into the long drawing-room.

The room had not been illuminated in years as it was that night.

Every wax taper was lighted in the silver candelabra, and the dim old mirrors multiplied their lights on every side. A great wood fire threw a cheerful glow over the portraits and the frescoed ceiling. All the linen covers had been taken from the furniture.

Lloyd, who had never seen this room except with the chairs shrouded and the blinds down, came running in presently. She was bewildered at first by the change. Then she began walking softly around the room, examining everything.

In one corner stood a tall gilded harp that her grandmother had played in her girlhood. The heavy cover had kept it fair and untarnished through all the years it had stood unused. To the child's beauty-loving eyes it seemed the loveliest thing she had ever seen.

She stood with her hands clasped behind her as her gaze wandered from its pedals to the graceful curves of its tall frame. It shone like burnished gold in the soft firelight.

"Oh, gran'fathah!" she asked at last in a low, reverent tone, "where did you get it? Did an angel leave it heah fo' you?"

He did not answer for a moment. Then he said huskily as he looked up at a portrait over the mantel, "Yes, my darling, an angel did leave it here. She always was one. Come here to grandpa."

He took her on his knee and pointed up to the portrait. The same harp was in the picture. Standing beside it, with one hand resting on its shining strings, was a young girl all in white.

"That's the way she looked the first time I ever saw her," said the Colonel dreamily. "A June rose in her hair, and another at her throat; and her soul looked right out through those great, dark eyes — the purest, sweetest soul God ever made! My beautiful Amanthis!"

"My bu'ful Amanthis!" repeated the child in an awed whisper.

She sat gazing into the lovely young face for a long time, while the old man seemed lost in dreams.

"Gran'fathah," she said at length, patting his cheek to attract his attention, and then nodding toward the portrait, "did *she* love my mothah like my mothah loves me?"

"Certainly, my dear," was the gentle reply.

It was the twilight hour, when the homesick feeling always came back strongest to Lloyd.

"Then I jus' know that if my bu'ful gran'-mothah Amanthis could come down out of that frame, she'd go straight and put her arms around my mothah an' kiss away all her sorry feelin's."

The Colonel fidgeted uncomfortably in his chair a moment. Then to his great relief the tea-bell rang.

CHAPTER IX.

EVERY evening after that during Lloyd's visit the fire burned on the hearth of the long drawing-room. All the wax candles were lighted, and the vases were kept full of flowers, fresh from the conservatory.

She loved to steal into the room before her grandfather came down and carry on imaginary conversations with the old portraits.

Tom's handsome, boyish face had the greatest attraction for her. His eyes looked down so smilingly into hers that she felt he surely understood every word she said to him.

Once Walker overheard her saying, "Uncle Tom, I'm goin' to tell you a story 'bout Billy Goat Gruff."

Peeping into the room, he saw the child looking earnestly up at the picture, with her hands clasped behind her, as she began to repeat her favorite story. "It do beat all," he said to himself, "how one little chile like that can wake up a whole house. She's the life of the place."

The last evening of her visit as the Colonel was coming downstairs he heard the faint vibration of a harpstring. It was the first time

Lloyd had ever ventured to touch one. He paused on the steps opposite the door, and looked in.

"Heah, Fritz," she was saying, "you get up on the sofa, an' be the company, an' I'll sing fo' you."

Fritz, on the rug before the fire, opened one sleepy eye and closed it again. She stamped her foot and repeated her order. He paid no attention. Then she picked him up bodily, and with much puffing and pulling lifted him into a chair.

He waited until she had gone back to the harp, and then with one spring disappeared under the sofa.

"N'm min'," she said in a disgusted tone. "I'll pay you back, mistah." Then she looked up at the portrait. "Uncle Tom," she said, "you be the company, an' I'll play fo' you."

Her fingers touched the strings so lightly that there was no discord in the random tones. Her voice carried the air clear and true, and the faint trembling of the harpstrings interfered with the harmony no more than if a wandering breeze had been tangled in them as it passed.

"Sing me the songs that to me were so deah
Long, long ago, long ago.
Tell me the tales I delighted to heah
Long, long ago, long ago."

The sweet little voice sang it to the end without missing a word. It was the lullaby her mother oftenest sang to her.

The Colonel, who had sat down on the steps to listen, wiped his eyes.

"My 'long ago' is all that I have left to me," he thought bitterly, "for to-morrow this little one, who brings back my past with every word and gesture, will leave me too. Why can't that Jack Sherman die while he's about it, and let me have my own back again?"

That question recurred to him many times during the week after Lloyd's departure. He missed her happy voice at every turn. He missed her bright face at the table. The house seemed so big and desolate without her. He ordered all the covers put back on the drawing-room furniture, and the door locked as before.

It was a happy moment for the Little Colonel when she was lifted down from Maggie Boy at the cottage gate.

She went dancing into the house so glad to find herself in her mother's arms that she forgot all about the new cloak and muff that had made her so proud and happy.

She found her father propped up among the pillows, his fever all gone, and the old mischievous twinkle in his eyes.

He admired her new clothes extravagantly, paying her joking compliments until her face beamed; but when she had danced off to find Mom Beck, he turned to his wife. "Elizabeth," he said wonderingly, "what do you suppose the old fellow gave her clothes for? I don't like it. I'm no beggar if I have lost lots of money. After all that's passed between us I don't feel like taking anything from his hands, or letting my child do it either."

To his great surprise she laid her head down on his pillow beside his and burst into tears.

"Oh, Jack," she sobbed, "I spent the last dollar this morning. I wasn't going to tell you, but I don't know what is to become of us. He gave Lloyd those things because she was just in rags, and I couldn't afford to get anything new."

He looked perplexed. "Why, I brought home so much," he said in a distressed tone. "I knew I was in for a long siege of sickness, but I was sure there was enough to tide us over that."

She raised her head. "You brought money home!" she replied in surprise. "I hoped you had, and looked through all your things, but there was only a little change in one of your pockets. You must have imagined it when you were delirious."

"What!" he cried, sitting bolt upright, and then sinking weakly back among the pillows. "You poor child! You don't mean to tell me you have been skimping along all these weeks on just that check I sent you before starting home."

"Yes," she sobbed, her face still buried in the pillow. She had borne the strain of continued anxiety so long that she could not stop her tears, now they had once started.

It was with a very thankful heart she watched him take a pack of letters from the coat she brought to his bedside, and draw out a sealed envelope.

"Well, I never once thought of looking among those letters for money," she exclaimed as he held it up with a smile.

His investments of the summer before had prospered beyond his greatest hopes, he told her. "Brother Rob is looking after my interests out west, as well as his own," he explained, "and as his father-in-law is the grand mogul of the place, I have the inside track. Then that firm I went security for in New York is nearly on its feet again, and I'll have back every dollar I ever paid out for them. Nobody ever lost anything by those men in the long run. We'll be on top again by this time next year, little wife; so don't borrow any more trouble cn that score."

The doctor made his last visit that afternoon. It really seemed as if there would never be any more dark days at the little cottage.

"The clouds have all blown away and left us their silver linings," said Mrs. Sherman the day her husband was able to go out of doors for the first time. He walked down to the post office, and brought back a letter from the West. It had such encouraging reports of his business that he was impatient to get back to it. He wrote a reply early in the afternoon, and insisted on going to mail it himself.

"I'll never get my strength back," he protested, "unless I have more exercise."

It was a cold, gray November day. A few flakes of snow were falling when he started.

"I'll stop and rest at the Tylers'," he called back, "so don't be uneasy if I'm out some time."

After he left the post office the fresh air tempted him to go farther than he had intended. At a long distance from his home his strength seemed suddenly to desert him. The snow began to fall in earnest. Numb with cold, he groped his way back to the house, almost fainting from exhaustion.

Lloyd was blowing soap-bubbles when she saw him come in and fall heavily across the couch. The ghastly pallor of his face and his closed eyes frightened her so that she dropped the little clay pipe she was using. As she stooped to pick up the broken pieces, her mother's cry startled her still more. "Lloyd, run call Becky, quick, quick! Oh, he's dying!"

Lloyd gave one more terrified look and ran to the kitchen, screaming for Mom Beck. No one was there.

The next instant she was running bareheaded as fast as she could go, up the road to Locust. She was confident of finding help there.

The snowflakes clung to her hair and blew against her soft cheeks. All she could see was her mother wringing her hands, and her father's white face. When she burst into the house where the Colonel sat reading by the fire, she was so breathless at first that she could only gasp when she tried to speak.

"Come quick!" she cried. "Papa Jack's a-dyin'! Come stop him!"

At her first impetuous words the Colonel was on his feet. She caught him by the hand and led him to the door before he fully realized what she wanted. Then he drew back. She was impatient at the slightest delay, and only half answered his questions.

"Oh, come, gran'fathah!" she pleaded. "Don't wait to talk!" But he held her until he had learned all the circumstances. He was convinced by what she told him that both Lloyd and her mother were unduly alarmed. When he found that no one had sent for him, but that the child had come of her own accord, he refused to go.

He did not believe that the man was dying, and he did not intend to step aside one inch from the position he had taken. For seven years he had kept the vow he made when he swore to be a stranger to his daughter. He would keep it for seventy times seven years if need be.

She looked at him perfectly bewildered. She had been so accustomed to his humoring her slightest whims, that it had never occurred to her he would fail to help in a time of such distress.

"Why, gran'fathah," she began, her lips trembling piteously. Then her whole expression changed. Her face grew startlingly white, and her eyes seemed so big and black. The Colonel looked at her in surprise. He had never seen a child in such a passion before. "I hate you! I hate you!" she exclaimed, all in a tremble. "You's a cruel, wicked man. I'll nevah come heah again, nevah! nevah! nevah!"

The tears rolled down her cheeks as she banged the door behind her and ran down the avenue, her little heart so full of grief and disappointment that she felt she could not possibly bear it.

For more than an hour the Colonel walked up and down the room, unable to shut out the anger and disappointment of that little face.

He knew she was too much like himself ever to retract her words. She would never come back. He never knew until that hour how much he loved her, or how much she had come to mean in his life. She was gone hopelessly beyond recall, unless —

He unlocked the door of the drawing-room and went in. A faint breath of dried rose leaves greeted him. He walked over to the empty fireplace and looked up at the sweet face of the portrait a long time. Then he leaned his arm on the mantel and bowed his head on it. "Oh, Amanthis," he groaned, "tell me what to do."

Lloyd's own words came back to him. "She'd go right straight an' put her arms around my mothah an' kiss away all the sorry feelin's."

It was a long time he stood there. The battle between his love and pride was a hard one. At last he raised his head and saw that the short winter day was almost over. Without waiting to order his horse he started off in the falling snow toward the cottage.

CHAPTER X.

A GOOD many forebodings crowded into the Colonel's mind as he walked hurriedly on. He wondered how he would be received. What if Jack Sherman had died after all? What if Elizabeth should refuse to see him? A dozen times before he reached the gate he pictured to himself the probable scene of their meeting.

He was out of breath and decidedly disturbed in mind when he walked up the path. As he paused on the porch steps, Lloyd came running around the house carrying her parrot on a broom.

Her hair was blowing around her rosy face under the Napoleon hat she wore, and she was singing.

The last two hours had made a vast change in her feelings. Her father had only fainted from exhaustion.

When she came running back from Locust, she was afraid to go in the house, lest what she dreaded most had happened while she was gone. She opened the door timidly and peeped in. Her father's eyes were open. Then she heard him speak. She ran into the room, and burying her head in her mother's lap, sobbed out the story of her visit to Locust.

To her great surprise her father began to laugh, and laughed so heartily as she repeated her saucy speech to her grandfather, that it took the worst sting out of her disappointment.

All the time the Colonel had been fighting his pride among the memories of the dim old drawing-room, Lloyd had been playing with Fritz and Polly.

Now as she came suddenly face to face with her grandfather, she dropped the disgusted bird in the snow, and stood staring at him with startled eyes. If he had fallen out of the sky she could not have been more astonished.

"Where is your mother, child?" he asked, trying to speak calmly. With a backward look, as if she could not believe the evidence of her own sight, she led the way into the hall.

"Mothah! Mothah!" she called, pushing open the parlor door. "Come heah, quick!"

The Colonel, taking the hat from his white head, and dropping it on the floor, took an expectant step forward. There was a slight rustle, and Elizabeth stood in the doorway. For just a moment they looked into each other's faces. Then the Colonel held out his arm.

"Little daughter," he said in a tremulous voice. The love of a lifetime seemed to tremble in those two words.

In an instant her arms were around his neck, and he was "kissing away the sorry feelin's" as tenderly as the lost Amanthis could have done.

As soon as Lloyd began to realize what was happening, her face grew radiant. She danced around in such excitement that Fritz barked wildly.

"Come an' see Papa Jack, too," she cried, leading him into the next room.

Whatever deep-rooted prejudices Jack Sherman may have had, they were unselfishly put aside after one look into his wife's happy face.

He raised himself on his elbow as the dignified old soldier crossed the room. The white hair, the empty sleeve, the remembrance of all the old man had lost, and the thought that after all he was Elizabeth's father, sent a very tender feeling through the younger man's heart.

"Will you take my hand, sir?" he asked, sitting up and offering it in his straightforward way.

"Of co'se he will!" exclaimed Lloyd, who still clung to her grandfather's arm. "Of co'se he will!"

"I have been too near death to harbor ill will

any longer," said the younger man as their hands met in a strong forgiving clasp.

The old Colonel smiled grimly.

"I had thought that even death itself could not make me give in," he said, "but I've had to make a complete surrender to the Little Colonel."

* * * * * *

That Christmas there was such a celebration at Locust that May Lilly and Henry Clay nearly went wild in the general excitement of the preparation. Walker hung up cedar and holly and mistletoe till the big house looked like a bower. Maria bustled about, airing rooms and bringing out stores of linen and silver.

The Colonel himself filled the great punch bowl that his grandfather had brought from Virginia.

"I'm glad we're goin' to stay heah to-night," said Lloyd as she hung up her stocking Christmas eve. "It will be so much easiah fo' Santa Claus to get down these big chimneys."

In the morning when she found four tiny stockings hanging beside her own, overflowing with candy for Fritz, her happiness was complete.

That night there was a tree in the drawing-room that reached to the frescoed ceiling.

When May Lilly came in to admire it and get her share from its loaded branches, Lloyd came skipping up to her. "Oh, I'm goin' to live heah all wintah," she cried. "Mom Beck's goin' to stay heah with me, too, while mothah an' Papa Jack go down South where the alligatahs live. Then when they get well an' come back, Papa Jack is goin' to build a house on the othah side of the lawn. I'm to live in both places at once; mothah said so."

There were music and light, laughing voices and happy hearts in the old home that night. It seemed as if the old place had awakened from a long dream and found itself young again.

The plan the Little Colonel unfolded to May Lilly was carried out in every detail. It seemed a long winter to the child, but it was a happy one. There were not so many displays of temper now that she was growing older, but the letters that went southward every week were full of her odd speeches and mischievous pranks. The old Colonel found it hard to refuse her anything. If it had not been for Mom Beck's decided ways the child would have been sadly spoiled.

At last the spring came again. The pewees sang in the cedars. The dandelions sprinkled the roadsides like stars. The locust trees tossed up the white spray of their fragrant blossoms with every wave of their green boughs.

"They'll soon be heah! They'll soon be heah!" chanted the Little Colonel every day.

The morning they came she had been down the avenue a dozen times to look for them before the carriage had even started to meet them.

"Walkah," she called, "cut me a big locus' bough. I want to wave it fo' a flag!"

Just as he dropped a branch down at her feet, she caught the sound of wheels. "Hurry, gran'fathah," she called; "they's comin'." But the old Colonel had already started on toward the gate to meet them. The carriage stopped, and in a moment more Papa Jack was tossing Lloyd up in his arms, while the old Colonel was helping Elizabeth to alight.

"Isn't this a happy mawnin'?" exclaimed the Little Colonel as she leaned from her seat on her father's shoulder to kiss his sunburned cheek.

"A very happy morning," echoed her grandfather as he walked on toward the house with Elizabeth's hand clasped close in his own.

Long after they had passed up the steps the old locusts kept echoing the Little Colonel's words. Years ago they had showered their fragrant blossoms in this same path to make a sweet white way for Amanthis' little feet to tread when the Colonel brought home his bride.

They had dropped their tribute on the coffin lid when Tom was carried home under their drooping branches. The soldier-boy had loved them so, that a little cluster had been laid on the breast of the gray coat he wore.

Night and day they had guarded this old home like silent sentinels that loved it well.

Now, as they looked down on the united family, a thrill passed through them to their remotest bloom-tipped branches.

It sounded only like a faint rustling of leaves, but it was the locusts whispering together. "The children have come home at last," they kept repeating. "What a happy morning! Oh, what a happy morning!"